For Charmaine —

When I was a kid
I read (from Jules
Verne) "Captain Nemo
went into the Nautilus
chamber and fell into
"Death's Twin Sister —
Sleep". Thus, this
book. Hope you
enjoy.

Robert

THE
SANDMAN

The Sandman

Robert Ward

TYRUS
BOOKS

F+W Media, Inc.

This book is dedicated to Ellie, Marty, David, Jay, and many of the doctors who helped me with the research. Because of bad nerves in the medical profession, none of them wanted to be named, but their help in the writing of *The Sandman* was crucial. I might add that most of them, once over the hump, described various possible methods of murder, lunacy, and other gore with a supreme joy. For that, I am most grateful of all.

Oh, Mister Sandman,
Send me a dream...
        Chordettes

THE
SANDMAN

1

Though he saw the light in front of him clearly blinking red, Peter Cross's foot did not hit the brake but the accelerator. A swarm of panic, like a shot of Methedrine, zapped through him and he could hear the squeal of brakes, the screams of a cabbie's voice.

"You fucking bum, wake up!"

Christ, Cross thought, not only do I nearly get my ass killed, but I have to put up with the cheapest sort of irony. For Cross had not been able to "wake up" for three nights. Not been able to, because he had not been asleep for three nights. More like thirty, fifty, a hundred, but he had stopped counting. Cross's rule: If he suspected that any time during the night he had dozed off at all, then that counted as a night's sleep. After all, studies made at the Blake Institute showed that incurable insomniacs, even the worst of them, always snatched some few hours of sleep, though they might not be aware of it. The problem was, Cross was aware of it; he couldn't swallow that soothing analgesic balm designed to "help the patient." For he suffered from an illness beyond the help of analysis—the Space, burning into his organs, opening him up like a great gutted fruit . . . He could feel it happening, his kidneys vanishing, his liver, his intestines, his heart.

He had been to a shrink once, and the man had tried to pry into him, to open the lid off the top of his handsome head and dig deep into the muck beneath his scalp... prying and peeping, such a good-natured creep with all the insight of a Roto-Rooter man. The Space was eating away inside of him... churning through his flesh... but he had to calm himself, for he was headed for work... he had to calm down.

"Hey, pal, you better shit or git offa the pot."

Cross turned and saw a pig-faced man with arms as pink and flabby as a baby's. The man's teeth gnawed at the air, and Peter suddenly felt nauseous and cold and very, very strange.

"You're driving on the street, pal," the man said, spittle flying from his mouth. "You better wake up... you unnerstan? You cut me off again, I'm gonna have ta do some damage."

Cross said nothing, turned away, and stared at the macadam.

The Bagel Nosh, the New York Furriers, P.J. Clarke's, they flew by him like images from a dream. *I cannot wake in the morning, I cannot sleep at night.* He thought of Poe, the stories he had started to read, and they seemed like imitations of his own internal state. The same images over and over, the cheap wallpaper of his parents' house on 21st Street in Baltimore; the pink roses peeling off of the wall, the hoarse bog of his mother's breathing, terrible pitching and heaving in the old creaked-spring bed, the medicinal odor (menthol) of the vaporizer, the beads of sweat on her forehead; the endless bottles of pills that did nothing to stop the cancer within her but worked only as a holding action against the encroaching pain, which ate away at her liver, her kidneys; she sitting in front of him with those moist deadpan eyes, sipping seltzer water, smiling and trying to tell him about Poe...

4

He snapped to at 58th Street, felt his flesh returning to him. It was like that with the Space—boring away at you and then suddenly gone, or there but not as noticeable. He had to slow it down, breathe normally, light a cigarette. Only two more blocks to the hospital. And a very tough day ahead of him.

The old woman, Lorraine Bell. Admitted yesterday, he had checked her stats, tried to get out of the room before her smell got to him. They had cleaned her, of course, but there was no hiding her smell. The rotting flesh. A gomer for sure. That was Harry Gardner's word, just another old piece of meat shipped from the nursing home, Windy Hills. Such a nice, pleasant name, and all the walls painted pastel to rest the old eyes, keep the old pulse level. But there was no slowing any of it down. Always going straight ahead, through the cutting edges of the morning. Always going straight ahead.

Except for her mouth, the way the lips curled up, as though she were in command of something—as though she were about to make a joke. There was a residue of beauty in her mouth. It had shocked him (and he recalled seeing the mouth last night, as he was pacing his apartment, walking slowly like a caged lion).

He turned into the 72nd Street entrance, went down the ramp, and felt as though he were riding along the surface of a tongue. A darting tongue which would flip him into the space marked in red, "Peter Cross Anesthesiologist." He stopped the Mercedes with a jerk, stepped out on the asphalt, saw the white shadow of a nurse walking toward the far elevator. Inside his chest he could hear something taking place. Stop that. You must stop. He crushed out the cigarette, adjusted his glasses, stooped down and looked at his thin, scholarly face in the window mirror. He noticed the slight blue bags under his tense slit-eyes. Like a serpent, he thought.

Patient's name Lorraine Bell. Moldy, wrapped in gauze.
With a joke about the mouth.

He walked from the elevator to the scheduling room.
Check and see if the patient survived the night. She had.
They were tough, very tough. Tougher than Harry Gard-
ner supposed.

"Hey, Cross, you got the gomer this morning?"

Harry Gardner stood in front of him holding his nose.
Peter stared at his huge, hairy forearms, the short, powerful torso and the stubs of legs. Harry looked like Popeye,
or an ape.

"Her name is Lorraine Bell, Harry," Peter said.

He could feel the beehive churning in him. Whirling
ghostholes through his body.

"The old bag is going to soil herself, Peter. Look out
when she lets the big load rip."

"Christ, Harry," Peter said. He started to turn away,
but Harry grabbed his arm. Peter felt as though there
were a branding iron on his flesh.

Then Harry cracked up and let Cross loose.

"Don't do that again," Peter said.

"What's this?" Harry said, taking a step back toward
Peter. "You getting tough?"

Peter stared at him, through him, and heard the sound
of stones being rolled.

"Good morning, Harry," he said.

"Space Cadet," Harry said. "You are the original Space
Cadet."

Peter heard his voice. It sounded small and far away.
He turned, went into the changing room, walked down
the rows of lockers, which suddenly looked as menacing
as the buildings on Third Avenue. He removed his pants,
neatly folded them over a hanger. Took off his shirt and
stared down at his well-muscled torso. He kept himself

6

slender, in shape, and yet he did not see that. He saw sagging flesh, the muscles being ground down by the years. He changed into greens, got his keys, slammed his locker shut, went into the hall, and stopped by A Room. Opening it, he stared at the shelves of briefcases, the other armamentaria of his colleagues. Here they kept their drugs, all of them—Rizzoli, Lampur the little Indian, Hernandez the Puerto Rican, Chung the Chinese, and Harry Gardner. He stared at their names taped on the bags. None of them was as good as he. Most were like Gardner, who only got into anesthesiology because he couldn't cut it at med school. Easy hours, good mobility, get stoned and laid on the weekends. He picked up his bag. Get ready for Miss Lorraine Bell.

She was eighty-one, blood pressure 160 over 60, with a joke around the mouth. Do your job, do it well . . . she is in pain and needs you. The doctors will find out where the bowel is obstructed. Though Peter thought he already knew. Her bowel would be obstructed from adhesions. Adhesions caused by other needless operations. He walked into the Ready Room, opened his armamentarium, and stared down at his drugs—plenty of neostigmine, succinylcholine, curare. He looked down at the long needle and thought of his mother, the injection heading into her arm. . . . Then he packed it all up and headed into the OR.

He was the first one in the room, and he busied himself checking over the anesthesia machine, making certain that the tanks of oxygen and nitrous oxide were set to the correct proportions. The oxygen content was all right—between 18 and 24 pounds per inch, but the nitrous oxide was a little low, so he raised it to 575 pounds per square inch. Then he turned as the two scrub nurses wheeled in Lorraine Bell.

"Hello, Peter."

Peter smiled at Debby Hunter, a tall, beautiful blonde, new to Eastern Medical. She smiled back at him, and he felt shy and looked away from her. He stared down but became aware of her legs, long and slender, and he thought of her standing there naked, no one else in the room . . . and the thought made the Space inside of him howl again, shift, hurting him.

He looked down at Lorraine Bell. Her face was lined with wrinkles—so many of them that he couldn't believe it. But there was the mouth—it seemed to be smiling— and it seemed to be young. He hooked the hoses up to the ceiling, green for oxygen, blue for nitrous oxide. He watched as Dr. Dios, the Filipino surgeon, came in. The doctor was a smooth, urbane-looking man, but Peter wondered what went on behind the mask. Now Dios began to kid around with Debby Hunter, ignoring the other nurse, Robin Hanlon, entirely. That was the way it always was. The good-looking, the beautiful, they got all the attention. The Lorraine Bells of the world got operations they didn't need. He looked down on her and was hit by such a surplus of emotions that he felt as though he would gag. He breathed in deeply again and checked the pop-off valve on the anesthesia machine.

"Peter, how have you been?" Debby Hunter smiled at him, and Cross felt his face flush. No goddamn good with girls. Never had been.

"I'm fine. Fine."

"That's good. Been reading much?"

"Why?"

"You looked tired. Besides, I see you reading at lunch hour. You usually have one of those ghoulish books of yours."

"Escape from the white tile womb," Peter said.

Debby laughed and helped Dios and the other nurse get Lorraine Bell onto the operating table. Peter went

8

back to his work, his pulse beating faster.

"Cross? Dr. Cross?"

"Yes?"

"How we coming?"

"Fine, just checking the vaporizer."

Cross poured a 150-cc. bottle of enflurane into the vaporizer, then turned and opened his armamentarium and began laying out his drugs—the 10-cc. syringe of sodium pentothal with 250 milligrams of the drug which would first induce Lorraine Bell to sleep, the 5-cc. syringe filled with 100 milligrams of succinylcholine which would relax her muscles, the 5-cc. syringe of curare used to maintain relaxation, and another syringe which he found himself reaching for as if he were in a dream, a 5-cc. syringe in which he placed 2.5 milligrams of neostigmine. He was barely aware of what he was doing. He began to shudder a bit . . . and laid out the atropine, 1.2 milligrams in a 3-cc. syringe. His tongue was dry, and he felt a cold chill come up his back. Across the room Debby Hunter talked with Dios, but he felt as though he were looking at her through a fog.

"Cross, Dr. Cross?"

"Yes. I'm coming."

He laid out the endotracheal tube, tested the rubber cuff on it by inflating and deflating the balloon. He then inserted the stylet into the end of the tube which would remain outside of Lorraine Bell's mouth. He lubricated it, softly rubbing the steel, rubbing it round and round, feeling, as he did it, clean and fast as though he were breaking out of a trance. He then checked out the laryngoscope to see if the light worked. He laid out oral and nasal airways and several tongue depressors to help the patient breathe. He wanted her to breathe for him. He wanted to feel her breath on his wrist. He checked her blood pressure chart again: 100 over 60. Still very very bad. Then he nodded to the nurse and let her know he was ready. He put on the blood pressure cuff, hooked on the leads for the cardiac monitor, made sure the IV was running properly. Lorraine Bell was now receiving her 5 percent dextrose and normal saline.

Quietly, fluidly, in a voice which sounded strange to him—it was that calm and peaceful—he said to Dios, "When she's asleep, I'll put in a central venous pressure line." Dios nodded and Peter took her blood pressure again. It registered as it had on the chart, 100 over 60, and her heart rate was 100, but irregularly irregular, which meant she was suffering from atrial fibrillation. In short, her heart was very weak, and he must be careful. Not too much anesthesia.

When he thought that, it was as if his mind had cleared and he was himself again—he felt brilliant, logical, scientific—the room had become all hard-edged chrome, steel, and tile, and the ecstasy and strangeness that had encircled him a moment ago were now gone. He felt "normal," though he didn't know exactly what that meant. But he did know that he kept right on feeling normal until the moment he put the 150 milligrams of sodium pentothal into the IV line. Then, out of the corner of his eye, he once again saw her mouth and he began to feel the fog sweeping over him.

Quickly he picked up the mask, put it over her face, and continued to hand-ventilate her with the bag. He watched as she went deeper, then he injected 60 milligrams of succinylcholine, and he watched as her muscles began their fasciculations, the fluttering of the eyelids, the rippling of the muscles in the arms and the knees, and finally the feet, jerking a little, then relaxing. He knew she was peaceful now, that all her pain was gone and that she was in the place beyond even dreams.

He inserted the laryngoscope into her mouth, exposed

10

the larynx, and placed the endotracheal tube down through the vocal chords into the trachea. He then removed the steel stylet from the other end and hooked up the connector to the machine. Carefully pressing the bag, he inflated the endotracheal cuff, checked for leaks, and, once satisfied there were none, he turned on the nitrous oxide and enfluorane mixture, still checking her blood pressure and keeping an eye on the cardiac monitor (he couldn't be too careful there).

He kept ventilating with the hand bag and secured the endotracheal tube with a loop of tape which went around her lips. When he touched them, something seemed to break inside of him, literally shatter, as though there were some delicate crystal goblet instead of organs inside his own body. But when it shattered, instead of pain, he seemed to be filled with a terrifically warm liquid, all at once clear and good, and he felt himself swimming in a kind of compassion.

Now he put in the oral airway, using a tongue depressor, and placed in an esophageal stethoscope which allowed him to listen to the patient's heartbeat and breathing. He checked the heart rate and noticed that during the induction it had gone up from 100 to 126, but now it was returning to normal. The blood pressure had dropped slightly, to 90, but he checked the intravenous line, inserted it, and took the pressure. He found it acceptable —"acceptable"—another word like "professional." Suddenly that word, too, made him feel wretched, and he began to breathe deeply. God, don't let anyone notice.

He put the manometer on the line—it read 9 centimeters of water pressure and was fluctuating well. She was ready now, and the circulating nurse prepped the patient's stomach with iodine soap. Debby handed the surgeon the sterile drapes and towels, and Dios draped Lorraine Bell. He did it quickly, professionally, and Cross felt as he always did when the patient was draped—cut off, removed from the operation. He had heard other anesthesiologists complain about it, especially Harry: "We get them all ready, we control it, and then they take over with their big egos and they get all the credit." With Harry it was all a game of power. Harry was sorry he hadn't been able to "cut it" in surgery. Dios now turned to Cross and nodded.

"May I begin?"

"Certainly," Cross said, and he liked the sound of his voice when he said it. Crisp, in control.

Dios wasted no time. He accepted the scalpel from Debby and made the first incision on the belly. His assistant, Dr. Black, clamped the skin off, and the operation was underway. It would take a while to find the obstruction in Lorraine's bowel. Since she couldn't tell them where she hurt, the obstruction could be practically anywhere. Dios had made the incision where another incision had already been made. Cross thought of the old adage he'd learned in medical school: "See an abdominal scar; think of obstruction due to adhesions." Surgery from the world of the blind. The patients knew nothing, the surgeon little more.

Cross was certain that Dios hadn't bothered to tell Lorraine Bell's children, if she had any, or if they had bothered to ask him. Probably they had not. Probably they had sent her off to a nursing home years ago, going out every week at first, then every couple of weeks, and finally once a month. By the second year they would call on her birthday and talk to a nurse, who would tell them she was doing quite well and "had taken her medication. Wouldn't it be a shame to wake her?" And, of course, they would agree... it would be too bad ... ridiculous to wake a now senile woman out of a good dreamy sleep. And so she would waste away until one day when

12

everything had fallen in—her cheeks, her nose, her eyes, one vast sag of wrinkles—everything gone except the mouth, as if it were fighting the battle all by itself, the battle to remain young and beautiful. Such a futile battle it was, too. Cross knew that. He was only thirty-five, but already in himself he could see the signs of decay. He stared over at Debby Hunter. God, she was beautiful.

He watched Dios and his assistant, Black, kneading Lorraine Bell's intestines, looking for fluid or gas trapped in the loops of the distended bowel. He watched as they shook their heads.

"It's not there," Dios said.

"I don't see any adhesions," Black said.

"This is so frustrating," Dios said. "If we can't find it, we'll have to open her up again."

"I know," said Black wearily, as if he had already given up hope.

Cross watched as she lay there; then he checked her heart, her blood pressure, her breathing. All okay, but then there was a sickening stench and the scrub nurse held her fingers over her nose.

"God," she said, "she's done it. She smells like dead fish."

The room reeked of Lorraine Bell's shit, and the circulating nurse, Mrs. Martin, looked as though she were going to pass out.

Now they were working on her abdominal wall, Dr. Black using the rakes and Kocher clamps to keep the wall open. Cross watched, still stunned, his left hand preparing to inject her with a slight taste more of anesthetic, this time curare if she became too light and began feeling the pain. (And also to allow her to stay at that great place he had put her. Yes, he was growing excited again, reaching for the syringe labeled Curare.)

He watched as they freed the small bowel from the anterior abdominal wall, dividing the adhesions which they found with dissecting scissors.

"Maybe these are it," said Dios. "Two adhesions. God, the last guy butchered her with the stitching . . ."

"Yeah," said Black, "but it didn't stop her from butchering us. Christ, that odor."

Cross watched as they began to cut through the adhesions. He knew that these two adhesions wouldn't be the last of Lorraine Bell's problems. Sure, they got rid of them, but from the looks of her, some young resident had been practicing carving turkey on her. How many more adhesions did she have inside the loops of bowel that Dios and Black didn't bother to plunge into because of the smell? It was clear from the speed at which they worked that they were doing their best to get out as fast as possible. Not that they were bad doctors—Dios was a bit of a hacker, but he was by no means the worst— it was just that everyone felt the same way. One had only so much time, stamina, and strength to waste on a gomer. Everyone knew she would be better off dead. So, given that premise, *anything* one did was sort of a bonus for her. Cross watched as the two surgeons started the Noble Plication, and he suddenly felt tears come to his eyes. God, don't let them notice. What was happening to him? Was he having some kind of crackup? He didn't understand it. But the moment he had seen her, something had clicked, and so now, as her body began to jerk a little from them tugging on her mesentery, he felt a cold chill come down his back.

He reached for the curare, with its pale green label, only he didn't pick it up. His hand reached for the neostigmine, and he had almost injected the drug into the IV when he noticed . . . My God, the wrong drug . . . or was it wrong . . . Lord, don't let them see. Slowly,

14

he put back the neostigmine, picked up the curare, and shot it into the IV. Six millimeters of it. Almost immediately Lorraine Bell began to relax. The doctors resumed stitching up the mesentery. The patient bucked, and now he felt a strange calmness descending over him. All the shakes and fears were gone.

He felt himself pulling away from everything, and he found his hand reaching for the neostigmine, the syringe with 2.5 milligrams in it, reaching behind the curtain where no one could see him (but then they couldn't see him anyway, for somehow they were no longer in the room, it was just he and Lorraine Bell, oh, yes, and he felt good . . . all of a piece, not split or unsure of himself anymore) and he stuck the 2-millimeter syringe into the IV, shooting the drug into it, then replaced it with the empty curare syringe, so if anybody looked, they would see nothing unusual, nothing unusual at all . . . and he heard his mother, Lila Lee, saying to him, "If I could just sleep through it . . . If I could only sleep through the pain . . . Petey . . . I could bear it if I could just sleep through the pain."

He checked her blood pressure. Christ, it was happening already. Her pulse rate had dropped off from 100 to 90 and was rapidly descending. Her blood pressure had dropped from 100 to 80 and was going down fast. Peter watched and felt the faintest sense of fear, a chill, but the chill seemed to be changed into something else, a rush of excitement, a spreading of happiness which poured through his veins.

Suddenly, Dios spoke up sharply: "Hey, Peter, there isn't much bleeding."

Peter turned and looked at the monitors (turned coolly, as if he had been preparing for this all his life).

"My God," he said, hearing his voice register a wonderfully accurate degree of shock and dismay. "Her blood pressure is down to sixty and her heart rate is down to fifty-five...and dropping...I don't know what the hell is going on! Stop the operation until I can get her stable."

Oh, he had done it. Just the right amount of "professional" concern.

Black's voice was urgent: "Her heart...ventricular heartbeats...now it seems...Christ, she's going into ventricular tachycardia...Shit...It's happening too quick...What the hell is it...she's going into V-fib...."

Dios nodded and yelled. (Though Cross couldn't hear him, he felt as if he had turned to gold. Never had there been anything like this. He had been waiting for this moment.) "All right, I'm starting external cardiac massage...Get the crash cart...We've got to get the pads on her."

Dios began to pump up and down on the heart, harder and harder, and Peter, feeling as though he were watching himself perform, began to give Lorraine 1.2 milligrams of atropine, which ordinarily would increase the heart rate, but he knew now that he had been successful. He had waited too long. The atropine would get to her too late...Oh, yes, as would the sodium bicarbonate, 50 milliequivalents worth he pumped into her, and finally the one milligram of epinephrine used to stimulate the pulse rate.

"It's not working," Peter said. "Nothing's working at all."

"It's no fucking good," said Dios.

"My God," said Debby. She turned her long, beautiful back to Peter and held her hair with her hands, like someone gripping the edge of a building. Peter watched her and felt another jolt go through him. He wanted to go over to her, put his arm around her, hold her face

16

and tell her it was all right. Everything was going to be just fine.

He stood there, hands limp at his sides, the glare of the hot lights reflecting off his glasses. He watched, deeply moved, as they wheeled the corpse into the hall.

He walked through his living room, hearing the sound of his stockinged feet as they glided over the fake Oriental rug. In his hand was a Scotch and soda, and the sounds of the ice cubes clicking sounded like the roll of dice on a back alley in Baltimore.

She was done. She was history, and he waited to feel ashamed, waited for the Space to start eating away inside of him, the rawness of the organs as the Space ate through him like an acid. He sat down heavily in his white chair, stared at the blank TV screen, and remembered the first time he had felt that way, sitting in his peeling wallpapered room on 21st street in Baltimore.

He had been staring across the alley at Rosalie Fangikis, the Greek girl, and she had started to take off her clothes. He watched her take off her sweater, toss her black hair back, walk to the window, and he felt himself getting excited—Christ how he wanted her. But then it came over him, the way his father had laughed at his skinny arms, the absurdity of his small chest, and birdlike legs. And he felt suddenly a wave of paralyzing self-loathing. It was nuts to even think of it. Not only was he not going to have Rosalie, but the fact was he was never going to have anybody. He was a mama's boy, Lila Lee's boy, the artsy crazy lady of the block. He began to shiver and to hold himself, wrapping his arms around his waist and moaning. It was then, at that moment, that the Space was born.

He felt hollow. He felt his heart, veins, kidneys, lungs disintegrating, like people disintegrating on Captain

Video serials. He squirmed on the cold, wide bed, and tried talking to himself—it's just a crazy feeling . . . it's all in your head . . . your heart is still in your body, you can hear it beating . . . your lungs are still there, you're still breathing. But the logic of his words didn't ease him. He felt empty, drained out, a non-person. He was never going to be alive, never going to be a man. He was a pussy. He couldn't even climb the fucking ropes in gym for Chrissakes. And when he turned and saw her body across the dark alley, he felt as though he were an empty goblet or a manikin. Push him over on the floor and he would shatter into a million fragments.

Now he sipped his Scotch, and looked around the room. The Space had never left him—never. He had tried to fight it, had finally, tearfully (and full of shame) told Lila Lee about his trouble, not actually mentioning the Space—he was too ashamed of that, too fearful of it to actually call it by name, at least to her—for even then he was aware that somehow she was partially responsible for it. She had taken him to Dr. Salem. He recalled the man's old office on Greenmount Avenue, the musty smell of old furniture and the dead glare of faded yellow lampshades. He had gone into the doctor's office and sat in front of the bald man, and after an hour of twitching and stalling, he could resist no longer, and he had broken down and told him about the Space—how he felt like nothing, how he would be on his way to school, and he would see a woman and he would feel it happening, the organs vanishing, smoking like dry ice. Eventually, after Peter had spilled himself to Salem, the doctor had asked him to wait in an adjoining room, and called in Lila Lee. Peter had sat by the door, staring down at a copy of Jack and Jill magazine. He sat quietly for a few minutes, and when the receptionist went to lunch, he crept close to the door and listened while the old man said things he didn't fully understand, "self-image," "hallucinations," "due to a terrible feeling of guilt and worthlessness," and hearing them made him even worse, for they seemed to be a death sentence, an actual confirmation of his most terrible fears. He was all these things. A "sicky," a "weirdo," a "nerd."

Then he heard his mother saying, "My son is not like that. He's just a little upset, that's all. How dare you label my son like that." And he had felt such tenderness toward her. She had taken up for him. She was his companion. The only one he could count on; and yet, yet wasn't it she who had made him that way? God, it was too terrible. He loved her, and yet when they left the office, and she tried to take his hand, he had violently pulled it away and then felt guilt for that, and inside him the Space began growing again, more violently now, like a jungle vine twisting around all his organs, smothering them, and it whispered a secret message to him, that it was never going to let him go—never—that he would pay for betraying it to that doctor, that he would always pay for the rest of his life. He was nothing, nobody, dead, no, worse than dead, he would be condemned to keep on living, while feeling hollow, scooped out, less than zero.

Now he got up and walked to the bedroom. Something strange was happening—something so new and delicious that he could barely understand it. He sat down on the bed, and with his right hand he touched his left bicep. It felt strong, full of muscle, and then he poked himself in the stomach. It too was all right—flat, muscular. God, he felt exhilarated, almost ecstatic. Those old memories of the Space, the persistent feeling of worthlessness which had never left him, never even after all these years, even after success as a doctor (For what was a doctor but a mama's boy grown up?)—suddenly the memories were simply that—memories. It was as though they were somebody else's life story, some poor, pathetic bastard who was lost and alone.

The Space had called to him and challenged him. He had met the challenge head on. He had killed—don't try and hide it—he had killed. He had taken the leap that every man, woman and child wondered about and secretly desired. (After all, what child hadn't thought about killing his punishing father, what poor working slob hadn't fantasized about doing away with a manipulating boss?)

He had killed and he felt good about it. He was alive, a man, and sitting there he felt powerful, aware of his own magnetic presence in the room. For the first time in his life he liked himself. He lay back, stared up at the ceiling, and he couldn't believe it—peace.

He was warm, very warm, and drowsy. And then, for the first night in years, Peter Cross fell into a deep, perfect sleep.

2

Dr. Robert Beauregard, chief of Anesthesiology, sat at the head of the long oak conference table and stared down at Dr. Dios and Dr. Black, Dios's assistant on the Lorraine Bell case. The long table, big enough for twenty, was where the department held its weekly morbidity and mortality meetings. During these inquisitions, any questionable deaths were discussed and accounted for.

Now with its seventeen empty chairs, the room seemed a melodramatic prop in a trial held in the Soviet Union for Crimes Against the People. At least Dios felt that way. He looked up, tried to meet Beauregard's gaze head-on, but it was impossible. Beauregard's power, his bearlike presence, was hidden beneath a shock of graying hair. His blue eyes were often penetrating, as though they were judging a man, even on the best of days, but during these meetings they looked cold, full of ice... Beauregard's obsession with unnecessary deaths was a legend in the hospital. Indeed, when they felt very good, some of the surgeons might make a passing joke about it. But not today, not sitting in the hot seat staring up at him. Beauregard had the lowest of burning points. He drove himself and his staff as hard as he could, and Dios had known from the very moment of Lorraine Bell's death that he was now on the shit list. Beauregard had said it over and over, "No unexplained OR deaths. They are unacceptable." Dios shuddered a bit, thinking of what a scandal could do to his career. He had come from a poor family in the Philippines, worked hard to get through med school, and was just starting to enjoy the fruits of his labor.

Dios's furious musings were interrupted by Cross's entrance. Peter swept through the door at precisely ten o'clock, a red scarf wrapped around his neck, his black raincoat unbuckled and swooping behind him like a cape. He looked, Dios thought, like some character out of the nineteenth century, very, very strange.

"Gentlemen," said Dr. Robert Beauregard in a voice that sounded as if it had come out of the grave, "let us begin. First, let me express to you my feelings on this matter. Lorraine Bell died during a bowel obstruction probe last night. You three men were the attending physicians. A human life was offered to you, put under your care, and you allowed that life to simply fizzle out. I can see from your looks that you're already angry at me for my tone of voice here. Well, I assure you that it's quite intentional. I don't accept the death of elderly patients at Eastern. As you know, I believe, and want you to believe, that older patients' lives are, if anything, more precious simply because their condition is more precarious. Every possible precaution must be taken to see that they do not have a shock reaction. Every possible gentleness and consideration must be standard operating procedure. I'm not talking about 'doing your job,' I'm talking about using *extra* caution, *extra* consideration. Now, knowing that, I want some explanation, gentlemen. I want some *solid, concrete* explanation. What the hell happened last night?"

Beauregard turned and looked at Dios, and Dios felt

22

himself burning with anger, felt his own heartbeat pumping up, as if he had just spent an hour jogging. Sweat formed on his forehead and he was afraid to wipe it off because he was afraid to acknowledge its presence. Sweat might be interpreted as guilt.

He had to say something. So he cleared his throat and began: "I needn't explain to you that the nature of the bowel operation was made more difficult because the patient was unable to tell us what pains she was experiencing. We opened her up and we checked the small intestine. I think that Dr. Black will agree with me that we took every possible precaution with Lorraine Bell's intestines. We handled her gently, as gently as possible. When we found the adhesion, we detached it. Again, we were extremely cautious. And when we sewed her up we were again very careful. I would say that we were *extremely* careful, wouldn't you, Dr. Black?"

Black nodded and looked straight at Beauregard. Dios welcomed Black's support, felt his breath come back in his lungs, and was able to swallow again.

On the other side of the table, Peter Cross remained motionless. He sat with his scarf still dangling insouciantly from his neck. His raincoat opened with a slash. His pince-nez glasses reflected the old brass lamp on the table. He heard Dios as though Dios were at the end of a long hallway, shouting to him through a broken bullhorn. He felt a wind sweep at his ankles and wondered why Debby Hunter wasn't there.

"What about the mesentery?" Beauregard said. "When you were sewing up Lorraine Bell..."

Dios, his confidence swelling, interrupted: "The woman had an irregularly irregular heartbeat to begin with, Doctor. We had a tough job with the mesentery. I'm sure you can appreciate that the tissue was already in an advanced state of degeneration. There was nothing much to work with. But we didn't put her under any abnormal strain."

Beauregard's eyes grew large and his right hand twisted into a fist. "According to whom?" he boomed.

"I don't follow you," Dios said, feeling the fear creep back in again.

"You said, Doctor, that you didn't put her under any 'abnormal' strain. And I want to know what your definition is. What is 'abnormal strain' in a case such as this? Are you telling me that according to the textbook, patient X received the legitimate amount of pressure?"

"No," Dios said, blundering forth. "I am not. I am saying that given this particular patient's advanced degenerative state, we had to work with the tissue for quite a while. But this is normal. We had to. And while I am talking, I would like to know why you aren't addressing some of these questions of yours to Dr. Cross, who sits over there and stares at us as if he were already absolved of any blame in this matter?"

Cross felt the words come as a blow to his face. For the first time he began to sweat. They couldn't catch him now. They couldn't blame him. And yet, there were two of them against him. He felt his back grow cold.

"Are you saying that I was to blame in this matter, Dr. Dios?" he said in a steely voice.

"Well," Dios said, "perhaps you can explain why the patient's heartbeat and breathing, given her condition, were perfectly normal one minute and dropped off violently the next?"

"I have nothing to explain," Cross said. "I spent the entire afternoon the day before yesterday preparing for my cases. If you'll check the records, Dr. Dios, Lorraine Bell had just been opened up two months ago . . ."

"I know that," Dios said. "You can't turn this thing around, Cross. I see what you're doing. Trying to make it

24

seem like I don't know my business."

Immediately Dios knew he had lost a point. He should have never used the word "business" there. He watched as Beauregard's eyebrows went up. Dios looked at Dr. Black, who quickly came to his assistance.

"I was talking to Harry Gardner this morning about the case," Black said. "He is completely neutral in his feelings and can look at it objectively. And he said to me that he was shocked by the way she started to fail. There was no indication that her heart was that weak."

"But it was weak," Beauregard said.

"Yes," Black said, "it was. We all knew it was weak and we were careful, but the way she began to go off, the way her pulse and heartbeat dropped so suddenly, was unusual."

Cross folded his arms and stared at Black and Dios. Fools, they were bungling it. Trying to pass off with innuendos. They would have been better to come right out and accuse him. But they didn't dare. Still, Cross was afraid, afraid they were getting through to Beauregard, and he knew he must rally.

"Unusual?" he said. "Unusual with both of you tugging on her mesentery until her whole body shuddered?"

"Is that true?" Beauregard said.

"That is a gross overstatement," Dios said. "Why don't you ask Dr. Cross about the amount of curare he used? I told him to keep her very light, yet I saw him, several times, add other drugs to the IV."

Cross looked at Beauregard, who was staring at him.

"You've got the list of the drugs I used," Peter said. "Perhaps Drs. Black and Dios would like to call an expert in to see if I acted properly. Someone as gifted as Harry."

Dios flashed a quick look at Black and shook his head. Beauregard looked at Peter Cross and nodded his head, giving a trace of a smile. Cross saw the smile and put on a grave look.

Before Beauregard could say anything, however, Black and Dios were at it again.

"He used succinylcholine... sixty milligrams... Perhaps that was a little heavy..."

Dios was waving his hands. Black was spitting out bits of saliva as he gesticulated. Each of them was revving the other up, ganging up on Cross. Peter began to shake; he could feel them moving in.

Then Beauregard slammed his fist on the table.

"Enough," he said. "Enough... I want both of you to shut it down."

Dios started to open his mouth, but Beauregard waved his index finger under his nose.

"Consider yourselves warned," he said. "I mean it. The way both of you have turned this around to make it look as if Dr. Cross is responsible is grossly unprofessional behavior. I have his report. I have gone over it and, given her condition, I think his judgment was fine. I would have recommended the same drugs myself."

Dios said nothing. He was drenched in sweat, but he stared across the table at Cross and felt a vast hatred. The truth is, Dios thought, I'd like to have an autopsy. But he didn't dare say it. Who knows what would come out of it. His own stitching job hadn't been that good. Maybe they would claim he had been too rough with her. So he said nothing.

"All right, gentlemen," said Beauregard, laying heavy irony on the last word. "I'm going to consider the matter closed. But that doesn't mean I accept Lorraine Bell's death as inevitable. Maybe you handled it perfectly and she died anyway. That can happen. But maybe some of you weren't thinking of the patient. Maybe you were thinking of her as a gomer."

Dios and Black winced.

"Remember, there are no gomers, there are only poor, old, sick people, and our job is to keep them alive and make them well if we possibly can. And before you go, I want you to know that though the matter is closed, I won't forget it. We've had a very low death rate on the operating table at Eastern during the last five years; less than ten percent. So that kind of death is simply not acceptable to me, and it shouldn't be to any of you. I hope I've made myself clear. Good morning, gentlemen."

After looking once more around the table at each of them, Beauregard slowly got up from his chair; the other three quickly followed his example and started for the door. Cross was a little slow in leaving, and Beauregard called to him.

"Peter, can I talk with you a minute?"

Cross turned and walked back toward the great bear of a man. Usually he felt like the others did around Beauregard—overwhelmed, intimidated. He also felt something else, something he had noticed the first day he had talked to Beauregard, the day of his hiring. A warmth, a realness, something almost chemical between the two of them. Impossible to explain. It bothered Cross, bothered him and at the same time pleased him.

"That was pretty rough, Peter," Beauregard said.

Cross smiled and nodded.

"Come, walk down to my office with me."

The two men passed out of the conference hall and strolled down the corridors of the great hospital. They passed several nurses and an old man in a wheelchair with tubes running from his nose. His skin was yellow, sagging from his bones.

"I want to ask you one thing," Beauregard said. "Then I won't mention it again."

"All right," Cross said quietly.

"Was there anything to what Dios and Black said?"

"I don't think so, sir," Cross said. "I feel as though I did the right thing. But I can't be a hundred percent sure."

"Does that bother you?" Beauregard said as they turned into his office.

"Yes, frankly," Cross said, moving carefully now, "it does. I spent most of the night awake, thinking about it."

"And?"

"And I decided I would have followed the same course again. I think I used all my skills. What bothers me is that I couldn't do a damned thing even though I gave it my best shot."

Beauregard was greeted by his secretary, Brigette. She sat by her telephone, a sandwich in one hand and *Dare to Love* in the other.

"Dr. Beauregard," she said, "I heard the sparks are flying."

"Is that right?" he said. "Eat your lunch and read your trash, Brigette. Thank you."

Both she and Beauregard smiled, and he led Peter into his inner office. Cross was surprised to see that the place lacked any semblance of order. Medical books were piled on his desk along with an art book on surrealism.

Beauregard noticed Cross staring at the book.

"A hobby of mine. I like painting very much."

Cross smiled. He was excited by finding out that Beauregard was interested in art. Especially surrealist art. For the surrealist writers and painters—Breton, Dali, Paul Eluard, and the others—had been the first great supporters of Poe's visions.

"I understand how you feel," Beauregard said. "It's not easy to lose a patient . . . but you can't afford to ever lose the capacity for caring and for hurting. I want to tell you something in confidence. I've been watching you, and I

28

think you have a remarkable ability. Not only within the field, but in your capacity for caring. I've heard good things from the patients, very good things indeed."

Cross felt a flush of excitement.

"You were ganged up on today because you're different."

He gestured at Peter's dark raincoat, his red scarf.

Cross stared at himself and laughed.

"I'm sorry," he said. "I'll try to buy some leisure suits."

"Lime green," Beauregard said. "Lime green is very chic."

They both laughed again, and Beauregard tapped his pencil on his desk.

"Well," he said, "I've got to get back to work. I just want you to know that I know you take your work seriously, and that whatever went on in there today doesn't change my opinion at all."

"Thank you," Peter said. He felt the rumbling inside of him.

The two men smiled at one another, and Cross felt as though Beauregard could look into him, see him quiver.

"I'll see you out," Beauregard said.

At the door Beauregard patted him on the back. His hand felt like it was radioactive, and Peter jerked back a little.

"See you, Peter."

"Right, Dr. Beauregard."

"Jesus, Peter . . . call me Beau. I'm not all that old and venerable yet."

"Of course," Peter said, smiling. But he did not add "Beau."

Beauregard watched him go down the hall, the way he moved, long, easy, graceful strides. The man had a natural dignity and style. Perhaps that more than anything else bothered the others. He walked back in his office and had just sat down when his phone lit red.

He picked it up and let out a deep breath.

"Dr. Beauregard,' said Brigette, "I have an important message for you. From Lauren Shaw."

"Yes."

"She's leaving two tickets for you for Thursday night's performance of her new play, *Charm's Way*. She said she expected you to make an appearance."

Beauregard thought of Lauren. Standing in front of him long, lean, and tanned, holding a champagne glass.

"Thank you, Brigette."

"Well? Are you going, Doctor?"

"Yes, I am."

"Ahhhh," said Brigette.

"Thank you for the news. Forget the exclamation points," Beauregard said.

He hung up and sat back in his chair. Almost any other man in New York would feel like celebrating, but his thoughts drifted to his estranged wife, Heather. He could still smell her on his sheets, hear her voice talking to Sarah. He felt a wave of loneliness and self-pity sweep him, and he wondered if the next time Heather called he wouldn't use the old "stay together for Sarah's sake" routine. No, he wouldn't—he hoped. He wanted to be honest and straight, but love had a way of making you lie. To your wife, but mostly to yourself. He hoped he would be strong enough to be honest about it. But it was a little like surgery; there was no way of really knowing what was happening until you began to cut.

3

Dr. Julio Dios and anesthesiologist Harry Gardner sat in the back booth of the Emergency Room Bar and Grill, one block south of Eastern Hospital. Above them on the walls were the instruments of their trade—masks, tubes, a giant comic needle three feet long, and a huge scalpel, big enough to cut open a giant. Harry Gardner picked up his Heineken's with his hairy hand and looked at the scalpel.

"Well, Julio, my lad," he said in a W. C. Fields voice, "when you see that scalpel, just what comes to mind?"

Dios, still smarting terribly from his disastrous morning, was able to give only a token laugh.

"It's not funny, Harry," he said. "I tell you, that Cross. There is not a doubt in my mind that he did something to that lady."

Harry looked doubtful.

"Now, come on, Julio," he said. "I don't like Cross any better than you do. And I've known him a hell of a lot longer."

"And?"

"And though I am loath to admit it, he's one hell of a smart dude. He knows his business better than any of us. That's the God-honest truth."

"That's not what I'm arguing about," Dios said, drinking his beer with a furious motion and spilling some of it down his chin. "Nobody's doubting his competency."

"Competency?" Harry said, incredulous. "I'm afraid he's a lot more than competent. The boy is a fucking genius. He blew everybody else out of the water at Cornell. I spent four—no, make that five—years in Ithaca with him and he was the whiz of every goddamned class. It got a little dull. Look, he's a cold bastard and the original Spaceman. I mean I wouldn't be surprised if he weren't some kind of goddamned closet case. Maybe he goes home all alone and eats boot polish, but the fact is, the guy is too good to make the kind of mistake you're talking about. Though I hate to stick up for him."

"You don't understand," Dios said. "I'm not talking about a mistake."

Harry stopped cold and looked up at the big needle on the wall.

"How do you mean?"

"I mean he was sweating, the same way I was sweating this morning. But unlike me, he had no reason to sweat. It was just a routine case. But he kept staring at that lady. It was weird."

"Well, you have to stare at the patient. You know that . . . just to see if her vital signs are okay."

"Hey," Dios said, lighting a cigarette, "whose side are you on?"

"Yours, boss," Harry said. "Just playing the devil's advocate. But I think you're dead wrong about Cross."

"You wouldn't be so sure if you had been there," Dios said. "There was something strange about it. He seemed to be fixated on her."

"And?"

"That's all. Admittedly it's not much, but I just have this feeling . . ."

Harry smiled. "Julio, old man," he said, running his

hand through his muttonchops, "I'll make a deal with you. I'll help you watch the creep. But between you and me, I think he's just got you psyched. As far as greasing somebody, Cross isn't the type. He doesn't have the guts it takes to wipe somebody. Hey, man, I know . . . I was in 'Nam for a year and I saw that kind of shit go down a lot."

"Saw what?" said Dios, looking shocked.

"I saw medics let people go," Harry said. "I saw worse than that. I saw them *help* people go, but it's not as bad as it sounds. These were boys with their balls shot off . . . no legs . . . with no fucking hope."

Harry sipped his beer and watched Dios's eyes. They were wide open in surprise.

"I saw it," Harry said, "and I never said shit."

Dios shook his head.

"I could never condone that, Harry."

"That's because you are a good, moral Catholic," Harry said, smiling. "But you weren't in 'Nam. In a place like that, you are playing by a whole new set of rules. Anyway, that's all water over the dam. What I'm saying is, I know Cross. He's weird. He gets obsessed with stuff, gets all caught up in it. But he would never have the guts to hurt anybody, much less grease somebody. No way."

"I hate that word 'grease,'" Dios said.

Harry called for two more beers, and when they came, he raised his glass and tapped Dios's.

Dios toasted and smiled and drank. He liked Harry. He was a real American—a he-man—but he just wished he wouldn't use that word "greased."

4

Nurse Debby Hunter sat in the small, concrete "park" which had been built by the hospital only the year before so that the staff might take advantage of the view of the East River. The park was a dismal failure, she thought. Not that they hadn't tried. There was a fountain with a boy and a dolphin in it that was supposed to be arty but looked vaguely pornographic. What was the boy doing with the fish, anyway? There were flowers in wooden troughs around the edge of the place. But now that fall was coming, they were dying fast and their drooping stems only made the place seem more gloomy than before. What really finished the place were the white concrete benches. Debby always felt the cold coming out of them when she sat down, the cold that ran right up her ass, through her spine, and into her neck. She dreaded the coming Christmas, living alone as she did on 77th Street and York Avenue in a singles' high-rise. That had been another mistake. She had only come to the city a few months before, after getting the job at Eastern, and the first nurse she met, Rose, had told her that the high-rise at 77th and York was a great place to live. "You'll never be alone. There are all kinds of professional men there. Hey, one of the Yankees even lives there, some relief pitcher. Anyway, it's a great place to meet men."

Debby hadn't really wanted to meet men as much as she had wanted to avoid being alone her first year in the city. And besides, she thought, coming from upstate (Syracuse—Debby had done her residency work at Strong Memorial), she had wanted to break some of what she knew were her provincial habits. For years she had gone through a tortuous relationship with an incurable playboy surgeon named Mark Schmidt, had put up with his unfaithfulness, his egomania, his ambition, and now she was ready for . . . well, she was not quite certain what.

Now, as she sat on the cold bench, eating a sandwich she had gotten out of one of the sandwich machines —a tunafish sandwich which tasted like it had been dipped in mercury batter—Debby thought of how easily the past had slipped by her. In a way it was frightening. Only six months ago she had been totally, irretrievably, hopelessly in love with Mark, and now she could barely recall what he looked like. Did that mean she was being turned into some kind of shallow, swinging-singles idiot? She doubted it, but then again, she wasn't sure. She wasn't sure of anything since she moved to New York. But she was sure that her fear of loneliness would be outweighed by her detestation of all the shag haircuts, hairy chests, Nik-Nik shirts, and golden pendants she had been witness to in the past few months.

Her thoughts were interrupted by noise behind her, and she turned and saw Harry Gardner following Peter Cross into the park. Before she could turn away, she saw Gardner give her the eye, and before she could gather up the wrappings from her sandwich and her empty juice carton, he was springing over to her. It was comical, really. She had just been sitting there, thinking of Mister Swinging Singles, and here he was, in the flesh.

"Hi, Debby," Harry said, his short, hairy arms hanging out of his green operating coat like those on a baboon.

"Hello, Harry," she said. "Have a good morning?"

"Yeah," he said, "a walkthrough, just a little hernia operation and a gallbladder, nothing the kid can't handle."

"Which kid are you referring to?" Debby said.

"The kid!" Harry said quickly, pointing to his own chest. "The kid, right here. Who else? Harry, the Kid."

"I've got to go, Harry," she said. "Lunchtime is over."

"Yeah, well, listen," Harry said, "your shift is off at five. So's mine. Why don't we go over to the Emergency Room and have a few drinks? I'd like to get to know you a little better."

"Oh, really, Harry? Get to know me a little better?" Debby said, putting Harry on.

But Harry was beyond irony. "Yeah," he said, "I would. I think you and I could maybe..."

"Make some beautiful music?" Debby said, overstating her sarcasm as much as possible so that he might possibly get injured and leave.

"Hey," Harry said, "give me a break."

"Sorry, stud," Debby said, "I didn't realize you were so sensitive."

"Hey," said Harry, "I'm not... I mean..."

"Yes?" Debby said. "What *do* you mean? Hmm?"

Harry stuttered and looked as though he were mortally wounded.

Debby heard a chuckle and looked over in the direction of Peter Cross, who had been left alone on the bench nearest the river. She hoped he might respond. In fact, she realized now that she had purposely delivered the last lines to Harry a little loudly so that Peter might hear her. There was something remote, distant,

36

and brilliant about him. The mere fact that a goof like Harry called him Spaceman (such an unoriginal, fraternity-boy putdown) had made her interested in Peter right from the start. But he had never shown the slightest interest in her. Or, if she could believe the gossip in the nurses' station, any other woman in the hospital. He was a real loner, which to Debby made him all the more attractive. But even now, she couldn't be certain he had laughed at her rebuff of Harry, because he was not facing her, but the river, and he seemed to be engrossed in a book.

"Look," Harry said. "You don't have to be so damned bitchy about it. Christ! I was just trying to get to know you."

"Harry," she said, "I am sorry. I just don't feel like it. All right?"

Harry recouped quickly. "It's all right, doll," he said. "Some other time. Well, I'll leave you now. Gotta go see some friends. You can stay out here with Dr. I. Q." He delivered the last line with some vengeance, then smiled and winked at her conspiratorially to let her know that she was a very small fish in his giant pond of guppies. She watched him as he bounded through the door back into the hospital.

Debby knew she should go in herself. She had her rounds to make, but the longer she looked at Peter Cross's back, the more interested she became. There was something about him that reminded her of a picture she had seen of an artist. No, not an artist, a poet of some kind. But she knew nothing of poetry. She had only thought of poetry because he was reading *The Collected Stories of Edgar Allan Poe.*

"Hello," she said softly, feeling terribly self-conscious, afraid that he would treat her as she had treated Harry.

For a second Cross did not look up. It was as if she

were invisible. Then he acknowledged her with a nod of his head.

"That was pretty rough in there yesterday," she said. "I hope they didn't get on you at the meeting."

He smiled a bit and shook his head.

"Not too bad," he said.

Now she smiled and sat down next to him.

"You're just saying that," she said, "but I can guess pretty well what happened. Dios and Black probably stuck up for one another. The surgeons always do."

He put his book down on his lap and nodded.

"Okay. You've got me there. But that's okay. Still it bothers me. I hate to see an old person suffer because some doctors want to test out their technique . . ."

"Do you think that's what happened?" Debby said, alarmed.

"Well, no, not this time," Cross said. "But the other times maybe. Do you know how many operations that woman had had in the past eighteen months? Five. And you know, four of them were probably the result of the first one."

Debby smiled, and shook her head.

"Dr. Cross," she said, "you are quite an outspoken person . . . I mean once you start talking."

"Really?" he said. "I always thought I was the Space Cadet."

Debby blushed a little. "You've heard those dumb jokes?"

"I've heard them."

"They make me furious," she said. "You know why people call you that? Because you're a little aloof and you like to read something other than junk. Like Poe."

"That's probably it," Cross said. "Too much for the conservative, soulless mind of science."

He chuckled a bit to himself, and she laughed with

him. He was much easier to talk to than she had imagined. In fact, he was charming. She looked at his book.

"Poe," she said. "I remember seeing a Poe play when I was a kid. They brought *The Black Cat* to our high school. Just a local group in Rochester. I watched it, and it didn't make any real impression on me—at the time, that is. Then later that night I went home and got in bed, and I began hearing the damned heartbeat under my bed. I mean it—it scared the hell out of me."

Cross looked at her in amazement. The simple story seemed to him a revelation.

"How did you feel?" he said.

"Scared," she said. "Very scared."

"Only scared?" he said.

"I don't see what you mean. No, wait, I do. No, there was something else. It was like I wanted it to stop, but part of me didn't. Part of me wanted to go right on being afraid. It was terrible, but it was deliciously terrible."

"Aha," Peter said, laughing. "Eureka."

He laughed wildly and touched her shoulder. She broke into laughter herself then and looked at his face. God, he was a handsome man, and strange.

"Poe will do that to you," he said. "There's no doubt about it."

They laughed a little more, but then neither of them seemed to be able to pick up the thread. She sat there for a second, a little nervous, tense, and waited for him to say something more, to ask for her number, but he just sat staring at her, and she finally had to get up.

"I'll be seeing you, Peter," she said. "I've got to get back to work."

"Sure," he said. "See you soon."

She moved away from him then, and wondered if he was attracted to her. And if he was, why he had blown his chance.

5

"You look as though you could use a cup of tea."

"Don't try subtlety, Mrs. O'Shea," Robert Beauregard said. "I look like I've been stuffed into a bottle of hydrochloride."

"Not that bad, darlin'," Mrs. O'Shea said, taking Beauregard's coat and hanging it in the closet. Beauregard looked down at his old Chippendale table and picked up the mail. Nothing but bills and requests for money from charity organizations.

Beauregard put down the mail and walked across the living room. What he saw depressed him. Not that there was disorder. Mrs. O'Shea had done a terrific job. His dark brown carpet and comfortable modern couches were spotless. His large glass coffee table was neatly stacked with magazines, and over in the corner, at the bar, all the ingredients for his vodka and tonic stood ready, including freshly cut limes. In the days before Heather had left him, he would have felt happiness that all this could be his. Especially the original Lyle Blackmore painting on the wall. An abstract in blues and yellows, with a jagged red line through its center, the painting had been Heather's purchase, not his own. She had seen talent in the young man from SoHo, whereas Beaure-

40

gard had initially only used the painting as an occasion to get off a good one-liner. "Looks like the price index graph at Con Ed." But now he had gotten used to that damned painting and he regretted his lame little joke. Perhaps that's why she had taken off to Europe—to escape his one-liners.

He mixed his drink, stared at the painting, trying to relax his brain in its cool colors. But his mind circled endlessly around Lorraine Bell's death.

Beauregard sipped the drink, and shut his eyes, and saw a hand reaching up toward him . . . a long, thin hand, like that of a concentration camp victim. He reached for the hand, and it grasped his wrist, the bony fingers clammy and cold. Then he looked down the length of the arm at the pathetically bony shoulder, and then at the two pale blue eyes which sat in the yellow flesh like two seeds—hard and flat and watery. The face was that of Kathy Albertson, one of his own patients . . . many years ago, when he was a resident. She had terminal leukemia, and her mouth was dry, small, and she was saying, "Doctor, please . . . please . . . ," and Beauregard felt terror growing within him, so that he wanted to rip the needles out of her arm . . .

"You ought to go to bed," said Mrs. O'Shea. "You ought to just take a nice nap."

"What?" Beauregard said, suddenly snapped back into his own home.

"You were nodding off," Mrs. O'Shea said. "You need a nap."

"No," he said, "I'm all right . . . really. I met an interesting young man at the hospital today. His name is Peter Cross . . . and he's really extraordinary. I was just thinking how Heather would like to meet him."

"Funny you should mention it," Mrs. O'Shea said. "Mrs. Beauregard called today from Paris."

"Yes?" Beauregard said, trying not to reveal the excitement he felt growing inside him.

"She said to tell you that she was coming to New York in a week or so. Maybe in time for the holidays. She wasn't sure of the exact date. She had to finish her studies first. She went on about her studies for quite a while, but I had no idea what she was talking about. To tell you the truth, she kept mentioning this fellow she had to study with, a man named Herman Neutics. Sounds like a real complicated lad."

Beauregard began to laugh out loud. It was the first time he had laughed all week, and the sound of his laughter seemed to come from a tunnel deep inside him.

"Mrs. O'Shea, you're a marvel," Beauregard said. "Hermeneutics is not the name of a man but a branch of philosophy."

Mrs. O'Shea shrugged and smiled.

Beauregard took a sip of his drink and sat down on the white couch. Outside he heard a siren sound... emergency... but his mind drifted toward an image of his wife... walking down the steps of the Lincoln Memorial... her yellow hair shining in the sun, her long, tanned legs outlined against the brilliant speckled concrete. A goddess... and like a goddess she was impatient... had to know everything at once. First philosophy, then English, then psychology, and finally Marxism ... God knows what she was into by now. She had always been quixotic, and it had irritated him. Just as his own steady course had bothered her. But now, as he thought of her, all his hostility melted away and he could only remember the good times they had shared at Georgetown—the nights working in the clubs, Beauregard playing piano, doing Mose Allison tunes. That seemed a million years ago... before she had been swept up by every revolutionary change the 60's had to offer.

She had come from money and had the natural confidence that money brings. She had never really wanted anything—unlike himself. He was from Atlanta, just as she was, but his family didn't have any real fortune.

Not for long anyway. Old Beau, his father, had been a successful GP but had blown the family money on several crazy investments—Health Food Chicken—a fried chicken with a batter made of megavitamins, and the Anatomical Robot, A Health Toy, which was designed to teach kids about the glories of the body. Unfortunately, the toy had been a bit too daring for its day, and the Southern Baptists had staged a robot melting party in Peachtree Square. By the time Beauregard had been ready to walk into the world, the money was spent. And he had to work in bars in Georgetown to pay his way through medical school. Still, they had been good days. He had met Heather, who was a psychology major. She had then switched to history, and finally, after they were married, had been converted to political theory. That was during the 60's, when every day had seemed like a new breakthrough. God, the people they had met... most of whom he had thought of as bums, hangers-on, or simply Heather-worshippers. But he had been wrong, and if she came back, he would show her that he could care, given a chance to do it his own way. He really would have to introduce her to Peter Cross.

"Sarah will be coming home soon, Beau," Mrs. O'Shea said. You better be getting a move on to eat dinner. I've laid out your tuxedo."

"God," Beauregard said. "That's the last thing I feel like wearing. And where is Sarah anyway?"

"Taking her ballet lesson, sir. She's a regular little

demon. She says she'll be in City Center in two years."

"And I will," came a voice from the door.

"Talk about timing, darling. I believe you will," said Mrs. O'Shea.

Beauregard looked up to see his blond, gracefully beautiful daughter smile at him. Her blue eyes, her perfect skin, her long thin face—she was already a beauty. Like Heather.

"Daddy," she said, racing across the room and kissing him.

He held her to him and kissed the top of her head. She even smelled like Heather, and he felt all his tenderness blooming forth from within. That and his intense loneliness. He sighed deeply and patted her head.

"Don't tell me to clean the room, Dad," Sarah said, as Beauregard tucked her into bed. "I already feel guilty about it, and I will devote all tomorrow morning to getting the books put back in the cases and the records back in the jackets and the dust from underneath the floor and the dolls put back on the dresser, and the lipsticks and powders put back into their containers, and all that other stuff."

Beauregard sat on the edge of her bed, smiled at her and shook his head.

"You, my dear, are . . . how would Mrs. O'Shea put it . . . ever so charming."

"I get that from you, Dads. I get being sloppy and other stuff from Mom."

"A lot of it is good stuff," Beauregard said, rearranging her quilt.

"Dad?" she said.

"Yes."

"Do you like Miss Shaw very much?"

"Yes," Beauregard said. "I like her very much."

"Oh," Sarah said.

"But not as much as your mother," Beauregard said. "I don't like anyone nearly that much."

"Oh," Sarah said.

Sarah laughed a little and picked up her copy of *Catcher in the Rye*.

"Next week she's coming back, Dad."

"I know," Beauregard said.

"Dad, do you think maybe..."

"I don't know," Beauregard said. "We still have problems. Big ones. But I hope..."

She squeezed him so tightly that he was shocked by her strength. He patted her blond head, and when she loosened his neck, he put his big hands on her shoulders and then wiped the tears away.

She sat back on her pillow, and Beauregard kissed her on her nose.

"Good night, Sarry. I love you."

"Love you, Dad," she said.

Then he shut the door and headed down the hall where Mrs. O'Shea was waiting with his topcoat. His hands and wrists felt as if they were prickled by needles, and when he looked into the hall mirror, he saw a face that was not a doctor's or a theater-going sophisticate's. He saw a father's face, and he thought it was the nicest and yet most frightening of all the other faces combined.

6

"I don't think we can get any closer, sir," the grad-student cabbie said apologetically to Beauregard as they pulled up half a block away from the Booth Theater on 45th Street.

Beauregard regarded the huge black limousines in front of him and shook his head. He was still tired from the day's trials at Eastern and he wondered if he shouldn't just tell Rodney Epstein, Interpersonal Development Major at NYU, to turn around and take him right back to his apartment. But then he thought of Lauren Shaw, her smile and her grace, and he smiled at Rodney and reached into his wallet.

"Thanks a lot," Rodney said. "Listen, I enjoyed sharing space with you."

"Right, pal," Beauregard said. "Your space is my space."

"Out of sight," Rodney said.

Beauregard shut the cab door and watched Rodney back into an alley and disappear. Funny, Beauregard thought, all the hell raised in the 60's about the New Consciousness and the only thing to come out of it was a lot of babbling, humorless nonsense about space and biorhythms. It made one recall the old line "full of sound and fury, signifying nothing," with a new respect for the Bard's wisdom. It had all seemed so damned profound at the time. Hell, he'd even tried a group therapy session on one of those marathon weekends with Heather. All that had been achieved was several levels of hysteria, and Beauregard had proved a terrific flop at hysteria.

Up ahead, Beauregard recognized Morris Blaustein, one of the principal backers of the show. Blaustein was a successful young lawyer, agent, and P.R. man, a kind of hip P. T. Barnum. Beauregard had met Blaustein through Lauren, and now he smiled at him, wondering if Blaustein would remember him.

"Beau," Blaustein said, moving through a group of tuxedoed men and signaling to the police to let Beauregard through.

"Hello, Morris," Beauregard said, shaking his hand. "Well, this is quite a night."

Blaustein smiled and shook his head.

"You'll like Lauren," he said. He emphasized the last word and then patted Beauregard on the back and went over to some more tuxedoed men who looked nervous. Beauregard recognized one of them as Billy Acton, the playwright. Acton was a big, lumbering guy and he looked ill-clad in a tuxedo. He was sweating profusely and his eyes darted to and fro, over to Marion Mott and Phillip Desmond, the critics for the *Post* and *Times*. Tonight, they were his judges, and Beauregard felt pity for the poor guy.

Beauregard watched as more limos arrived and more stars appeared. Each one of them got a special greeting from Morris Blaustein. Beau found himself enamored of the whole scene. Tonight was fun, a good night. Enough of the hospital, the sick, the dying, the hopeless, the stupidity and arrogance of the surgeons. Lord, let him relax and have a good time. He reached into his pocket, pulled out his tickets, and went inside the theater and directly to his seat.

Morris walked down the aisle toward Beauregard and sat down next to him. Beauregard felt both delighted and wary. Blaustein never did anything without a motive.

"I'm really glad you could make the play tonight, Beau," Blaustein said, in his suede voice.

"Yes, it's just what I needed."

"Just what Lauren needed, too," Blaustein said.

"How's that?" Beauregard said.

"Well, I don't have to tell you that she's become very, very fond of you. She seems a little stage-struck."

Beauregard managed a laugh.

"Come on. Lauren and I are . . ."

"Just good friends?" Blaustein laughed. "I know. But she likes you very, very much. She gets so tired of show people. Everybody wants a piece of her now that she's making it big. And it's not easy for her to turn them down. She's a very generous person. But it takes a lot out of her."

Beauregard got the distinctly unpleasant feeling that he was being led somewhere, somewhere he had been led before. By patients who feared the worst.

"Has she been tired?" he said.

"Very," Blaustein said.

His voice was grave, and yet even as he delivered the bad news, he saw another theater critic, Joyce Katel of the *News*, and he managed a sparkling smile and a gay little wave.

"She complains of head pains."

"Headaches?"

"Well, yes, I suppose," Blaustein said, "but she calls them head pains. She says she knows what a headache feels like and this isn't it."

48

"Hmmmmm. Depression. I'll have a talk with her."

"Good," Blaustein said. "After the show we're having a cast party at Sardi's. It's probably nothing, Doctor; she hasn't done Broadway for some time and she is most likely going through that whole footlight trauma . . . you know . . . they never outgrow it."

"Good Lord," Beauregard said. "I should say not. I wouldn't want to be up there."

"No?" Blaustein said, smiling. "I was just looking at you when we were standing outside, thinking how easily you could be cast as a noble, caring doctor."

Beauregard laughed and Blaustein smiled at him, and then the overture to *In Charm's Way* started.

After fifteen minutes of *In Charm's Way*, Beauregard understood that it was what Morris Blaustein had once described to him as a "percentage play." That is, it was a totally commercial enterprise with just the right percentage of sex (not really sex at all, but mere titillation), just the correct percentage of mystery (Who had stolen Lauren's priceless Degas?), and just the right percentage of laughs, which were mixed with the correct, civilized amounts of empathy. In short, the whole thing was a formula, tried and true, without a striking or original note in it. He propped his head up on the seat, composed his face in the receptive expression he felt necessary, and caught the first act. Lauren entered and he applauded loudly. God, she was beautiful, but he worried about her. She pushed herself too hard. In many ways they were alike. Both of them caught up by their careers to the point of maximum stress overload. That wasn't good—it made for a constant, gnawing need to work, which in its own way was worse than a gnawing need to make money or achieve power. It hemmed you in, narrowed you. That was what he had really wanted to say to

Cross . . . that you had to have time for people, had to go easy on yourself . . . then Lauren's voice, as though it were far away, and in a second, in spite of his best efforts, he fell sound asleep.

"I'm so glad to see you, Beau," Lauren said, smiling at him and pouring him a glass of champagne. "So very glad."

He stood at the open French windows of Sardi's upstairs room and looked down on the glittering lights of Manhattan. He took Lauren's hand and pressed it tightly. Her hair was jet-black, her eyes beautifully hazel, and her complexion tanned and smooth as a child's, though he knew she was thirty-five. Her body was firm, her breasts perfectly full and rounded, her waistline so tiny he knew he could pull her to him like a child. Yet, her legs were hard, long, a woman's legs, and he thought, My God, my God, I'm here with one of the most desirable women in America and yet . . . Yet, there was something missing, some intimacy that he shared with Heather, that he felt he might never share with anyone else, and it made him feel tense, coiled inside.

"You were terrific in the play," he said, before she could ask him how he liked it.

"Really, Beau," she said, smiling at him and kissing him gently on the cheek. "Please don't you be as sycophantic as the others. We both know it's utter garbage."

Beauregard smiled. She was utterly charming and without a trace of self-deception.

"Do you think it will be a hit?" he asked, trying to sound optimistic.

"Of course, darling," she said. "Of course it will. It has the right blend. Low comedy, bad dialogue, and ersatz romance. It can't miss."

"What's this I hear about romance?" said a voice behind Beauregard.

He turned and stood face to face with the most beautiful redhead he had ever seen. At least ten years younger than Lauren and wearing a dress cut down to her navel, she seemed to pulsate with sex. Beauregard actually felt startled looking at her.

"Oh, God," Lauren said. "Just when I was beginning to kid myself into thinking I was young again."

"Oh, you are young," the woman said. "Younger than springtime . . ."

She smiled and started to sing the song from *South Pacific*.

"This," said Lauren, "is Lynne Carter. She is newly arrived in New York from the Coast. And if the reaction of the men in this room sets any precedent, I would say that she will have Mayor Koch sitting at her feet within twenty-four hours."

"Just give me some work," Lynne said, taking Beau's hand. "Robert Beauregard?" she asked.

"Yes," Beauregard said, "but how . . ."

"The papers," Lynne said. "I have nothing to do between cattle calls but read the papers. Let's see, this week you were in Liz Smith, Page Six, and Suzy's column. That's not bad. You must have hired Morris to do your P.R."

"That's terrible of you to say," Lauren smiled. "Beau doesn't like publicity, and if you remind him of it, he'll surely race back to his germs and microscopes . . ."

"No, no," Lynne said, grabbing Beau by the arm, "he's the first male I've met all night who doesn't have a beard, a shaved head, and tight pants. You mustn't leave."

"Well, if it's that serious," Beau said, "I might be induced to spend a few more minutes with you two poor ladies."

"Oh, do . . . please do . . ." said Lynne, mocking panic.

Lauren and Beau both laughed, and Beau watched as Lauren tilted back her beautiful neck. Like Ava Gardner's, Beau thought, getting a bit high from the champagne. Then, with no warning, Lauren Shaw began to fall. Her glass dropped from her hand, and she collapsed toward Lynne and Beau. Lynne dropped her own glass and grabbed her arm, while Beau quickly got his arms around her waist.

A crowd started to form, but Beau moved them back. Lauren had come to almost instantly and leaned between Lynne and Beau.

"It's all right," she said. "It's all right . . . Just this opening-night tension."

"How do you feel?" Beau said, motioning Lynne toward a chair near the buffet.

"Dizzy . . . a little dry in the mouth. I'm all right. Just nerves. And my head is aching like hell."

"Here, sit down," said Lynne.

She and Beau slowly lowered Lauren to a gold brocaded chair.

"I feel fine," Lauren said. "It's just a guilt attack. The artiste feels the pangs of remorse for playing in crap."

Beauregard looked at her eyes.

"Follow my finger," he said.

"Really, Beau," Lauren said. "This is not Dr. Kildare time. You'll make the backers nervous."

"To hell with the backers. Just look at my finger."

She did as he said. He watched her pupils carefully, and they tracked him easily.

"I see a huge ugly octopus," Lauren said. "I see giant cans of Liquid Plumber . . ."

"Cut the comedy," Beauregard said. "How long have you been having these headaches." He took her pulse, which was up to 140.

"A couple of weeks," she said. "It's nothing new . . . I

have had them for years."

"Morris told me that you felt that these pains were different from ordinary tension headaches."

"Oh, Morris . . . he's the ultimate Jewish mother. No . . . it's exactly the same. I feel fine . . . though it is a bit close in here. Why don't you get my coat and take me away from all this?"

She blinked melodramatically and waved her arm pathetically as if she were a true damsel in distress.

Both Beau and Lynne laughed and shook their heads.

"You are impossible," Lynne said.

"Yes," Lauren said, getting up and smiling brilliantly, "I am, dear . . . but that is the privilege of stardom."

So saying, she took the coat Beauregard offered her, flipped it over her shoulder, tossed back her head, took Beau's arm, and headed for the door.

"Oh, Miss Shaw," Lynne said, in the voice of a stage-struck little girl, "how you do carry on."

As the limousine sped past the lights of Broadway, Lauren Shaw moved across the back scat and put her head on Beau's shoulder.

"You okay?" he said.

"I am now," she said, looking up at him.

"Fine," he said, with a slight edge to his voice.

"My, that was a professional sounding 'fine,' " she commented.

"Well . . . it wasn't meant to be."

She reached up and playfully boxed his ear.

"Poor, poor Beau," she said. "I don't know why I throw myself at you. You know I staged that whole thing just to get you away from Lynne Carter. I saw you staring at her fantastic body. I heard the wheels turning in your head."

Beauregard smiled and held her hand tightly. "You are impossible."

"I suppose I am," Lauren said. "It's just that I am so lonely . . . you know it is *terribly lonely* at the top." She batted her eyes like Bankhead.

"Give me a break," Beauregard said.

Lauren smiled and snuggled up next to him.

"I hope you'll come in, Doctor," she said. "I'm beginning to feel faint again."

Beauregard looked down at her, smelled her perfume. Silently he damned himself for being old-fashioned.

"Heather," Lauren said.

"Well? I mean . . ."

"I feel so faint," Lauren said, snuggling closer to him.

"You'll be fine," Beauregard said. "All you need is a good night's sleep."

The car pulled up to her home in Turtle Bay. Beauregard thought of her hanging gardens which would be bathed in moonlight . . . a glass of champagne . . .

But before he had a chance to weaken, she was up and out of the car.

"I'm not going to ask you again, Beau," she said, this time in a sincere voice. "Because I know that you can't deny me three times in one night. However, when you get that woman out of your head . . . do come and see me."

Beauregard smiled and shook his head. She reached back down, and he kissed her fully on the lips. He knew that if he was going home at all, he better make his move now.

"My driver will take you home, you dear fool," she said.

"If those headaches come back," Beau said.

"I know who to call."

She squeezed his hand, winked at him, and then shut the door, and Beauregard watched her recede as he sped away into the night.

54

7

He was cold, and his eyes were filled with crust. He got out of the damp bed, damp from the sweat which had dripped off his icy body, and grabbed his water glass. When he put it to his lips, he suddenly felt them burning, and he jerked it away in horror. Then got up and looked at himself in the mirror. There was nothing on his lips and he wondered if he wasn't losing his mind. "Nobody ever died from insomnia," was what all the doctors said. But nobody ever talked about going mad from it. Nobody ever talked about waking up and feeling that one of your arms was gone, or feeling that the room was coming in on top of you to smother you like a big piece of dough.

He walked around the bed and slipped on a magazine, almost fell down. Jesus, let this night end... let it end ... Why couldn't he sleep. It had been fine for a couple of days there after Lorraine Bell... It had been fine... But now, now... It was back again. The feeling that the Space was calling to him again. The Space that he could never quite get full... He wandered into the living room, found his bathrobe lying in a heap on the floor. He picked it up, put it on, took out a cigarette from the pocket, and found his matches lying on the TV. He stared down at the TV... the huge eye which you watched all night, over and over, but which might be watching you . . . Ridiculous thought . . . calm down . . . but at four in the morning no thoughts were ridiculous. You were in the land of dreams, even though you weren't asleep . . . He looked out the window, heard the wind howling . . . and saw someone hustling down the street, his rain-coat flapping in his face. Yes, he thought, get home—get home fast, where it's safe . . . Only he knew that it wasn't safe anywhere. There was no place you could really get away from what was inside of you.

He turned on the TV, but the light blinded him, and after one minute of a Popeil's Pocket Fisherman ad he turned it off. Next they would have on Vegematic . . . It slices and dices. He walked back through the hallway and went into the kitchen. Opened the refrigerator which seemed to be humming abnormally. He stared into it at the butter, which looked like a huge yellow brick, the tomatoes, and the waxy, dead-looking green peppers. He poured himself some grapefruit juice and sat down at the kitchen table. His temples ached and his hands shook. God, he had to stop this. He started to drink the juice when he saw a roach run across the table. He was startled by the bug, terrified by it. It was almost as if he were see-ing it in 3-D. It was huge, its brown antennae hanging over the white table like some long, filthy membrane. He wanted to crush it, but somehow was afraid of it. Then he brought his hand down on it hard and watched it squish, and he started to laugh loudly . . . He hated the sound of his own voice, the laughter was not that of joy but of panic. He heard the Space whirling inside of him, and it seemed to cry out that it needed to be filled . . . it needed it desperately, and he shook so badly now that he was spilling the juice.

He got up and ran back into the bedroom. Sat down on the edge of the bed and called Debby. He had memorized her number, though he didn't know why. He hadn't even thought about it consciously. It just happened naturally, and he let the phone ring three times.

Finally she picked it up ... He heard her voice ... Yes, it was her.

"Hello ... hello ... Who is this?"

He wanted to say something. He felt like a fool. It must be three A.M. She would think he was crazy.

"Hello, who is this? Hello?"

He put the phone back on the hook and lay down on the bed, and stared up with wide, blue eyes at the rippling, buckling ceiling.

8

Esther Goldstein got out of the elevator on the seventh floor of the Riverside Apartments. As she stepped into the hallway, she suddenly felt a sharp pain in her left arm—a strange, circulating spasm which shot around her neck and landed like an arrow near her left breast. She put down her heavy suitcase and leaned on the wall. Though she was fifty-eight and had felt the pains twice in the last month, she didn't panic. If there was one thing she was not going to be, it was a Jewish mother. She was all through with that, had been since Morty died, and she had started analysis. Let people laugh, if they wanted, but her shrink, Dr. Gruenberg, had changed her life. She was a loving, caring, sensual person. *Oy gevalt*, if Morty could see her now, having an affair with a gentile weight-lifter named Big Ned Malloy. They had met at a YMHA dance and it had been love at first sight. She sighed and headed down the bland white-walled hallway toward her son's apartment. Barty would never understand this . . . any of it . . . her lover or her new look . . . her fashionable Ralph Lauren hacking jacket and corduroy skirt, her tall Jourdan boots . . . her wide silk tie . . . but he was simply going to have to get used to it . . . After all, this was a new, modern world where people were free to live out their fantasies, and why shouldn't they? If Barty wanted to stand down by the Big Board and read ticker tape all day, that was his business, but such a life? You might as well be eating stale bagels ... and if they thought for one second she was going to let them ruin little Morty's life ... her only grandson ... and turn him into a *nebbish* like his father, well, they just didn't know Esther Goldstein. As she approached the door, she sighed heavily and felt a little twinge of pain again ... probably nerves. With a cocky jab, she pushed the button to her son's apartment. In a second, the door opened, and there stood a squat man with a head like a cauliflower with hair. His little eyes blinked in surprise and his hand ran up to his chest, where he patted the reindeer which was stitched on his sweater.

"Ma," he said. "Ma ... Hey, Betsy, come here quick. Look who we got at our door. Annie Hall."

Peter Cross wheeled his patient, James Thomas, out of the operating room. Thomas, a forty-eight-year-old insurance actuary, had just successfully come through a colostomy, and though Peter had given him a shot of morphine just as the operation ended, there was little doubt that James Thomas was going to be in a great deal of pain when he awoke. He thought of the same man just the other day, sitting up in his room, talking about getting back on his local bar's basketball team ... "the over forty league," he had laughed.

Peter stared down at him ... at his huge, hulking body ... the kind of kid who used to scare him on the playground, who punched him because he couldn't climb the ropes in school, the kind of kid he had wanted to be. He kept his hand over Thomas's chin to keep the airway patent. He could feel Thomas's breath on his palm—yes, the breath was there, jerking but there—and Peter felt as though he were being drawn out of himself, into

Thomas's body. He was staring right at the wound, the lacerations, and he was surrounded by Thomas's membranes; the blood pulsated in Peter's ears, and he felt something happening inside him, the Space crying out, wanting to be filled. He looked over at the nurse on duty ... He saw the surgeon ... Carpenter, waiting for them.

"How's he doing?" Carpenter said.

"Fine," Peter said, amazed that his voice sounded normal, for he could feel it inside him, swirling around like a screaming, whispering snow.

"Time to wake up, Mr. Thomas," Peter said as they wheeled him into his place behind the curtain.

Thomas didn't stir.

"Come on now, Jim," Peter said, lightly slapping his face. "Time to wake up."

Now Thomas began to come out of it a bit.

"He'll be fine," Peter said. "Just fine."

"Sure," Carpenter said. "Sure ... okay, I've got another one right away ... This is sheer lunacy. Can you handle this, Peter?"

"No problem," Peter said.

Carpenter smiled and nodded good-bye, and Peter stood there looking down at Thomas.

"Yes," Peter said. "You're going to be fine... Fine..."

They were all around him—just outside the curtain. He reached into his pocket, felt for the syringe ... Funny, he wondered why he had stuck it in his coat after the operation. The feeling wasn't even conscious then ... He smiled at the idea ... He was getting his responses directly from the patients now. Cross rubbed the syringe between his thumb and forefinger. He took it out ... hearing the chatter of the nurses and other doctors in the Recovery Room. He stared down at the syringe. Curare, a good, quick shot. He held Thomas by the arm.

60

"Has anybody seen Peter Cross?"

Peter jammed the syringe back into his pocket. He felt a cold sweat break out on his face.

"In there? Oh, thanks..."

He breathed in deeply and started to tap Thomas lightly on the side of the face.

"Okay, Jim. Time to wake up. Okay, Jim."

"Well, hello."

Peter looked up and saw Debby Hunter staring at him. She was dressed in a pair of tight Levis and a pink sweater, and had her sunglasses on top of her blond hair. She looked smashing, and he felt unable to speak.

"How's he doing?" Debby said.

"Fine," Peter said. "He's doing just fine."

"Terrific," Debby said. "How are you?"

"Okay," Peter said. His mouth was dry, and he thought of her voice at 3:00 A.M.... He felt weak.

"Listen, Peter," she said. "I don't ordinarily do this kind of thing..."

She laughed and sucked in her breath.

"No?" Peter said, managing a smile.

"God, that's the oldest line in the world. But it's true, I really don't ordinarily ask a man out. I like to think they'll ask me. But...anyway...I know you are a big Poe fan, and there is this Poe revival up at the Eighty-Sixth Street Cinema. I think it's two pretty good ones. *Pit and the Pendulum* and *The Premature Burial*."

Peter stared back down at his patient, who was showing signs of coming to.

"There...that's good, Jim. That's good."

"He's okay?" Debby said.

"Yeah," Peter said, in a voice so upbeat it surprised him. "He's okay and I'm off...and, ah...I've got a very attractive date tonight."

Debby sighed.

"Well, I tried," she said.

Peter walked toward her and smiled.

"So if you'll just go down to the cafeteria for about ten minutes while I scrub up . . . we can get going."

Debby smiled and squeezed his arm.

"Terrific," she said. "But if I faint, you've got to promise to bring me around."

Peter laughed, turned James Thomas over to the Recovery Room nurse, and sat down at the little table to finish his tally of the drugs he had used during surgery and the amount of blood lost. As he wrote, he looked over at Debby, who was talking to another patient. God, she was beautiful . . . long and lean . . . and she had asked him out. He reached his hand into his pocket, ran his thumb and forefinger over the syringe. Then he got up, motioned to her that he'd be down in a minute, and hurried on down the hall to the locker room.

9

"God, I'm sorry," Debby said as they left the theater.

But for Peter Cross, there was nothing at all to forgive. They had come into the theater too late for the first feature, but *The Premature Burial* had been exciting. Not that it was really any good. He agreed with Debby completely, the production was not much better than an old B-movie. But the scenes in the casket, the look on Milland's face as they shoveled him into the earth, had contained real moments of genius, Peter thought. More important, seeing the images made his own impressions all the more vivid. He took from the scenes what he wanted, automatically and unconsciously filtering out the rest. The experience had been thrilling from beginning to end. And her presence there beside him ... that, too, had been thrilling, though he didn't know if he could tell her any of this.

They found themselves on the corner of 86th and Lexington, staring through the hazy, drizzling rain at the traffic lights and the pink marquee of the shop across the street.

"Well," Peter said, "I'm famished. How about you? Would you like to get something to eat?"

"Yes," she said, "I would. I'm hungry too."

They crossed the street and Peter started to go in the

coffee shop but suddenly changed his mind. He knew a little French place on Third Avenue. He hadn't ever been there, but he had heard Dr. Beauregard talking about it one day. It was a crazy impulse, not like him at all. Ordinarily he paid very little attention to food, but tonight was different.

"Look," he said suddenly. "Let's get a cab. I know a much better place."

"Sure, Peter," she said happily.

He stepped out into the street to hail the Checker, and she took his arm.

The place was called Ça Va, and they found themselves a table in the back, beneath some hanging blue flowers. She smiled and took off her coat.

They ordered quiche and white wine, and Peter found himself talking. It happened suddenly. Right in the midst of his wondering if he could talk, he simply began, and he found that she was listening, really listening. The impact of this was too much for him, and he talked on.

"You know," he said, "it wasn't really bad. I mean they tried hard to capture the whole ambience. You were right, I did enjoy the sets and the costumes. They had things right. And that scene where he was buried, that was well done. It was fun for me."

"See," she said, "life isn't all chemicals and gases and dying patients."

Peter went on as if he hadn't heard her.

"But they missed the point with Poe, you know. I've never seen a production that really got the point at all."

"What is the point?" she said. "I thought it was simply to scare the hell out of you."

"Do you really think so?" Peter said.

Debby was aware of him staring at her. There was such intensity in his eyes, and a glittering intelligence.

64

But more than that she saw something else—a hunger which ran so deep that it frightened her, and turned her on. She knew he wanted her, but at the same time he seemed to be pulling away by challenging her.

"Maybe there is more there," she said, running her hand through her hair and smiling at him.

He smiled back.

Now he seemed positively carnivorous, and she realized that to Peter her intelligence was a measure of her sensuality. He could never go for a dumb broad just for the sex. And she found herself wanting to be as smart as he wanted her to be.

"There is a kind of sensuality to everything Poe writes," she said, sipping her wine and smiling at him. "I know that was mixed up with it . . . the tremendous excitement I felt as a child reading his stories. It was an excitement that seemed to come from deep inside of me."

"Yes," Peter said. "Yes . . . that's exactly how I saw it."

He was excited now . . . he couldn't help himself. Here was a girl—no, a woman with brains—and the sensitivity to understand his feelings toward Poe. She had the same feelings herself . . . God, he wanted to blurt things out to her as she sat across from him looking so fresh and perfect. The way the candlelight danced over her skin. Such soft skin . . . he wanted to put his hand across the table and touch her face, but he had to control himself. Still, she was smiling now . . . and his eyes dropped to her full breasts, which were made all the more appealing by her tight sweater. But it wasn't merely physical—no, it was that she understood, she really did . . . he could teach her the rest . . . maybe he would risk it . . . .

"You have experienced him," Peter said. "You've really felt what's there . . . the way I used to feel it when I read the stories to my mother . . ."

He stopped. He had never told anyone about that. He

knew he shouldn't go on. But perhaps she could understand, and he stared at her breasts again . . . until he became embarrassed by the length of his silence.

"Tell me about your mother," she said.

"Well . . . we lived in this row house in Baltimore. My father had a sign company . . . he wanted to be an artist . . . and my mother acted for a while . . . she was quite beautiful, actually . . . I mean she was a beautiful person . . . not merely physically beautiful . . . she read and wrote poetry . . . but they had very little money . . . and then she got sick . . . cancer. She was only in her early forties, but she looked much younger. She seemed as young . . . and as fresh . . . as you. I mean that's how I remember her . . ."

She smiled and drank her wine. Her face reflected in the crystal, and then he was talking, talking compulsively . . . she had such luminous blue eyes . . . he thought that Poe himself would have loved to see such eyes . . . and it had been so long since he talked to anyone about anything that mattered.

And when he was finished, Debby was smiling at him so warmly that he found himself basking in her friendliness, her loveliness, and he placed his hand on hers.

"Peter," she said softly. "I feel very close to you . . . very close . . . Oh, I shouldn't say that."

"No," he said. "It's all right. I understand. I feel . . . the same way."

"It's just that I've been so lonely," she said. "I've met so many people like . . . like that imbecile Harry Gardner . . . I know what you mean. It is almost as if they have had something cut out of them. All they can respond to are bright colors . . . football games . . . comic books . . . they seem all lively on the outside, but underneath you can see them."

"The dead soul beneath the living skin," Peter said.

"Yes," Debby said. "But you're not like that. You're
an extraordinary person."

He found himself drawn to her so overwhelmingly
that he wanted to hug her right across the table. Then he
felt fear, but he told himself that it was all right . . . she
was exquisite . . . perhaps since he had finished with
Lorraine Bell he was more in tune with others who could
share his own unique way of life. But he would have to
take her along slowly—very slowly. Still, God, she was
there, smiling at him, almost begging him.

"You live nearby?"

"Yes, Peter."

"I wish . . . the night didn't have to end," he said.

"It doesn't," Debby said, taking his hand as they got
up from the table.

"No," he smiled, helping her on with her coat. "Why
should it be over. There's no reason for that at all."

As they walked through the lobby of Debby's building,
Cross felt a terrible tightening in his stomach, a strange
seizure of panic and near hysteria. What was he doing?
Perhaps she had hypnotized *him* in some way—not with
her mind—no, he was certain he was smarter than she,
but with her body, her eyes, her breasts, and her legs. He
saw her legs as she walked a couple of steps in front of
him. Perfect, so damned perfect. He wanted her. He
wanted her badly, but there was something happening
inside of him, a voice telling him to stop right now.
Beware. He tried looking away from her at the tiled
walls. There was a mosaic of a man and a woman walking
through a field of grass. God, it was tacky, tacky and
cheap. He followed her dutifully, like a small child, to
the elevator, and again he was overcome with the sensation that he wanted to bolt, but she looked at him and
smiled, and he found himself smiling back. He felt the

67

warmth spread through him.

She held his hand. The elevator arrived. Two men with blow-dried hair, tight red-and-blue body shirts, and huge gold link necklaces got off and brushed by him. He felt the sickness return. Why would she live here if she wasn't one of those kind of people herself? Wasn't it obvious? She was just another one of—what was it Harry called them? Hitter Chicks. Yeah, the Hitter Chicks, exactly like the ones who hung out in the café across the street. Only she was better at it, had put on a face filled with upstate shyness and innocence, and he had fallen for it, told her all the stuff about Poe, about his mother. Things he hadn't ever meant to tell anyone. Now he was trapped in her apartment.

He began to feel sweat pouring from his neck and a grime-and-gut-wrenching slime in his groin. She had taken advantage of his loneliness. He wouldn't forgive her.

The elevator stopped and they stepped into a narrow hallway painted with bright yellow flowers. Tacky. Horrible. Why hadn't he bolted? But he kept walking with her, a step behind. He kept his eyes on her ass and her neck. God, she had a beautiful neck. Even now, raging with fear and resentment, he knew that he was going to go with her. He had to.

"Here we are," Debby said, slipping her key into the lock.

She pushed open the door, walked assuredly through the dark room, and switched on the light.

"This is it," she said, smiling and opening her arms as if to offer him the room.

Cross looked around. There was a feeling of warmth in the apartment unlike his own black-and-white-and-chrome. Debby had fixed the place up with a warm blue couch, an old-fashioned bookcase, two very comfortable-looking overstuffed chairs with deep blue corduroy covers. Hanging from the walls were plants, and in the fireplace were real logs. On the floor was a very tasteful Indian rug. It had a design on it—a cherry tree harboring two peacocks. So she did have taste—eclectic taste, but taste, sensibility. Perhaps he wasn't wrong to confide in her. He had to calm himself, not dwell on things.

"Would you like a drink?" she said.

"Yes. I'll have a Scotch."

"Johnny Walker Red?"

"Fine."

"I think I'll have a Campari and soda."

She walked around to the kitchen, and again he found himself following her. But he stopped at the bookcase. There were a couple of novels, mostly Book-of-the-Month Club stuff, but there was also *The Collected Illustrated Stories of Edgar Allan Poe*. He took out the book and looked through it. The pages looked fresh, unmarked.

"Did you just buy this?" he asked.

"Yes, Peter," she said. "I just did. And if you want to know if I just bought it because I met you, the answer is partly yes and partly no."

She smiled seductively, warmly, and handed him a drink. Then she went and sat down on the couch. He followed her there. He felt foolish. He wondered if she knew that he felt as though he were following her around like a puppy. God, if she did, he couldn't stand the embarrassment of it.

"I mean I do like you, Peter. I sensed it that day we had lunch. And tonight I've had such a wonderful time. I have to admit that liking you was what prompted me to buy Poe. But it wasn't only that. It was what you said the first day about the experience. I had repressed that whole part of my childhood, the terror of being young and insecure, of feeling so out of it all the time. The Poe thing had something to do with that too. So after I talked to you, I got the book because it reminded me of things I had forgotten."

Though he didn't show it, Peter felt astonished. She was just about the best-looking woman he'd ever seen, and here she was, talking about her horrible childhood, of being "out of it." He didn't trust her. It was scarcely possible. Yet she seemed honest.

"I would have thought," he said, holding his drink rather stiffly, "that anyone who looks like you do would have had an entirely satisfactory childhood."

"Oh?" she said. "Thank you for the compliment, but it was murder. You see, I came from a working class section of Syracuse. I don't know if you've ever been upstate, but you might as well be in Alabama or some place like that. There is tremendous ignorance there, a provinciality. People don't like little girls to be smart. And I didn't look like a girl at all, or at least I didn't look like what the ads tell us teen-aged girls are supposed to look like. I had buck teeth, fixed by braces. I had bad skin, which fortunately didn't scar. And I had big breasts on a small body. The boys used to grab at me and then laugh because I screamed. I was good at science, I was good at math, but in those days it was considered ridiculous to even think about medical school. Besides, my parents couldn't begin to afford it, and I didn't do that well in my other subjects. I didn't do well because I was upset a lot of the time. I couldn't concentrate. I don't know why I'm telling you this . . ."

"No, I want you to tell me," he said. "I want you to, because I like you. I knew it from the first moment we met. I really did."

They moved toward each other on the couch and he took her in his arms. When they kissed, he felt as though

70

he were in a cheap movie. It was that thrilling, all the more so because it seemed so innocent, so touching. Underneath that woman's body she was a little girl really. He would teach her. He held her to him, his heart beating wildly, and he kissed her again. This time she opened her mouth, tentatively, and he felt shocked, surprised. Now she was suddenly a woman and he wanted her, wanted her terribly, but even as he thrust his tongue into her mouth, he felt the fear coming over him. But now she was moaning softly, and he felt his hand rubbing her large, firm breasts, felt the nipples sticking straight out, and she started calling to him, again and again, "Peter . . . Oh, Peter . . ." and he was terribly excited, but afraid. What if she was an experienced woman? What if he disappointed her? God, he hated his long stringy body. He hated it. When he shut his eyes, he tried to imagine that he was someone else, someone with a body like a movie star, strong, with good muscle definition. He had gone soft. He should have worked out more often. She'd be turned off when he took off his clothes.

He rubbed her and felt his cock harden, and then his hand went under her and he felt her thighs, and she was gasping and heaving and saying his name over and over again. He felt like he was going to burst, but he also felt afraid, terribly afraid. He shouldn't have let it go this far. No, God, no, he shouldn't have let it. He didn't even know her. She could destroy him. And so, suddenly, he was unable to control himself. He pulled away.

"My God, Peter, honey, let's go into the bedroom," she said, still panting, her jeans pulled half down. He saw her hard, bronzed thighs, and he began to tremble. He felt as if he were going to cry.

"What's wrong?" she said. "Is there anything wrong?"

"No," he said too loudly. He sounded as if he were angry with her.

"Then come on to the bedroom with me. Please, Peter."

She was leaning over on him now, and pulling up his shirt, licking his stomach. He began to feel like he was going to be sick.

"I just don't feel well," he said. He hated the sound of his voice. Why couldn't he take her? God, she was beautiful, and she did like him.

"Relax," she said, lifting her head and staring at him. "You know you're a very sexy man. You just need to relax. I think you've worked so hard that you've forgotten how to relax."

"Maybe," he said, but he felt miserable. He had lost his erection and had almost convinced himself he was sick to his stomach.

But she was holding out her hand and he took it, and, as if in a dream, they were walking into the bedroom. She sat him down on the end of the bed, knelt below him, took off his shoes and socks, then rubbed his feet. She began unbuttoning his pants, all the while repeating his name, "Peter, Peter." He felt his ass lift and he lay back on the bed, staring into the darkness. She told him to relax, to just think of anything, and he felt her mouth close on his cock and he felt himself harden, and her head was going back and forth, and he gripped the sides of the bed. She was making murmuring noises of joy.

He lay there, feeling the sensation coming from his groin into his stomach. Oh, God, it felt good, so very good. Then he pulled her up to him and she straddled him. Now her jeans and panties were off. She came down on top of him, and as he went into her, she screamed out his name. Together, they began to rock to and fro. She was crying and holding him, and once again he was struck by how warm and giving she was, by how much this meant to her, not merely the physical sensation, but

72

how much she wanted and needed him. Though the voice inside him whispered, "It's cheap. She's just hungry for it, anyone would have done," he knew it wasn't so. She could have been here with anyone—a girl with breasts like hers and that flat, tanned stomach and the golden pubic hairs and her pussy riding him, sending shuddery wave after wave of pleasure through him—she could have been here with cocksman Harry, who undoubtedly was far superior to Peter, who knew all the little tricks, but she wasn't. She was here with him, Peter Cross. So in spite of the voices inside him hissing away, he was enjoying it and giving it to her as she gave it to him, until neither one of them was thinking about anything any more. They both burst forth with a scream of elation and joy.

"That was so nice," she said. "Oh, God, that sounds ridiculous. That was good, no, that's not it. It was beautiful."

Peter held her to him in the dark.

"You're beautiful," he said. "You're beautiful."

"And you are."

"No," he said, "I'm out of shape."

"Uh, uh," she whispered.

She put her leg over his and kissed him on the head.

"I like you very, very much," she said. "Maybe I like you too much."

He stroked her hair, ran his hand down her perfect back and over her ass. In a second she had fallen asleep, and he lay there waiting to join her. But it didn't happen. Instead, the voices started again, the fears and the doubts. "So you had an orgasm, you felt something in your body. Is that all it takes to make you forget? Is that what you can be bought for? Is that all it takes?"

He tried not to listen. He tried to pretend he was a

happy, satiated lover, which in part he was, but there was the other part, like teeth inside of him. When he looked down on her sleeping figure, he saw her differently —once again like a sleeping animal. She had hungered. She had eaten. And now she slept. He shut his eyes, felt the Space moving inside of him, starting to whirl about . . . then he touched her ass, laid his hand on the base of her spine. He sighed deeply. He felt inordinately tired, exhausted, fading out. But still, he did not sleep.

10

"Listen to me," Esther Goldstein said. "I'm telling you it's nothing."

"I'm sure it isn't, Ma," Barty said, as the cab sped across town toward Eastern. "I'm sure it isn't, but you've been having those pains for two days now and you *know* about your heart condition."

"I don't believe this," Esther said, knocking the peacock feather away from her face. "I get to Bloomingdale's twice a year and my worrywart son is rushing me off to the emergency room of a hospital. I mean, *oy*—"

She didn't finish the last sentence. The pain had intensified and was shooting up and down her left arm. She felt short-circuited.

But mostly, even as she suffered from her heart, Esther Goldstein's main sensation was one of embarrassment. She had come to show them how she had survived, by God. She had come to be an object lesson for Barty who was prematurely aging and had started to play it safe full time. And now, oh God, the pain was getting worse. Perhaps she should have listened to Dr. Benson in Cincinnati, when he suggested that she not try to get in shape too quickly. But no matter what it was, no matter how bad the pain became (and there was no let-up), she

75

was going to pull through this. She knew it. She was dead certain.

"We're here, driver," Barty said. "Don't get out, Ma. I'm getting a stretcher."

Esther tried to get up, but she was beyond that stage now. She stared out the window of the cab and made out the name Eastern Medical. In less than two minutes they had wheeled her through the crowded halls of the Eastern Emergency Room. Her nervous son and shell-shocked daughter-in-law tried to keep up with the residents who rushed her along.

"To think," Esther said, "twenty minutes ago I was in Bloomies."

"Mrs. Goldstein," said a fat nurse, "you must try and keep quiet."

"Keep quiet?" Esther said. "Keep quiet? I might be dying. And if that's the case, I'll have years to keep quiet."

But the pain hit her again, a great nauseating wave of it, and for the moment she wasn't able to speak.

They wheeled her quickly by the nurses' station and then by the anesthesiologist's Ready Room.

"Some ride," Esther Goldstein said, as the pain cut back a bit.

A couple of the residents even laughed at that one. Their voices caught Peter Cross's attention as he was checking out his armamentarium. He looked up and saw the frizzy-haired lady staring at him, with enormous eyes. He smiled at her and snapped shut his case and headed off to the cafeteria for lunch.

They wheeled Esther Goldstein into X-Ray, and then into the Cardiac Monitoring Room, and two doctors attached the electrocardiograph machine to her. She looked down at the electrodes on her chest.

"Look, Barty," she said, "I'm the bionic yenta."

Above her, a round doctor named Tompkins, with a nose that made him look like Mr. Potato Head, began talking to another doctor, a short man with small, slit eyes.

"This woman needs a coronary bypass operation," Tompkins said. "I think it's as simple as bypass, two months in bed, and she's as good as new."

But the shorter man, Dr. Snyder, waved a small, eloquent finger in the air. He looked as though he was conducting an orchestra.

"Not a chance," he said. "Her color is good. She's awake, and her pulse isn't too bad. I'm not at all sure we can't treat her medically."

Tompkins turned and pulled out some X-rays they had just worked up on Esther.

"Look at these, will you?"

"Forget it," said the short man. He stared at his own fingers as if he were transfixed.

"That's right, Doc," Esther gasped. "Forget it. I've seen better acts than yours on the Gong Show."

"Good," said the little man, patting the fading Barty on the arm. "We'll get you into the Cardiac Monitoring Unit . . . work up some tests. We'll get her ready for the angiogram. There's nothing to really worry about. We've caught this in plenty of time."

"You're sure she's going to be all right?" Barty said.

"Absolutely. It's the best unit on the floor. We've got around-the-clock nurses and closed-circuit TV. Any problems arise, we nail them down in a minute. Nothing will go wrong."

Barty took out a handkerchief and rubbed his head.

"Trust me," the doctor said.

11

At precisely 3:00 A.M. Harry Gardner began to feel the urge come over him. It was always that way with Harry. Go out, snort a little coke (and what was that stuff cut with?—Drano?), have a few drinks and maybe smoke a joint, and see if he could score... If not, he would try and go to bed, but by that time he would be too jacked up to sleep... and he would feel a great, gaping horniness... a need... for something... anyone to keep him going. Now he stood outside of the nurses' station, watching June Boswell walking toward him, holding her patient's chart and a tray of pills in Dixie cups.

"Hi," he said.

"Harry... I told you... I don't want to see you."

He stared at her large breasts, her thick hips, her full, sensual lips. He usually went for thinner women, but there was something very ripe about her... at least now. He remembered an old country song, "When I'm half shot, you're not half bad."

"Harry... I'm very busy."

"Come on, June... You already made your rounds. Everybody is sleeping like a baby."

"Harry..."

Her voice was small, pleading. He knew she couldn't

resist him. She loved it . . . the sex and the risk of being caught.

He leaned on the glass wall and looked in at the cardiac monitors.

The tapes with the EKG readings of the patients were folded neatly out into trays. Harry walked over and picked up one of the pieces of tape and ran it across his lips.

"June," he said, "you know I've really been wanting to fix some of those old anesthesiology machines in Room Two-twenty-two. Why don't you come down with me?"

"Harry," she said, smiling, "I can't. Yvonne is helping Dr. Frost with a cut-down, and Rodgers and Hargrove are out taking a break. Somebody has got to be here to check on the EKG readings. What if one of the patients had a problem?"

"Come on," Harry said, moving behind her and kneading her back muscles with his strong fingers. "How likely is that to happen? Besides, if anything does go wrong, we'll hear the squawk box. And we'll come right back. And what's more . . . if we don't do it now, we blow it for the entire night, because as soon as they come back . . . well, you know it wouldn't be good if anybody saw me here."

"What's the matter?" June said. "Worried about your professional reputation?"

She patted his hand and then gave out a long, self-satisfied sigh, and got up from her chair.

"Well," she said, "I don't suppose I should send you down there to fix those machines all by yourself."

As June and Harry walked down the hall, Peter Cross walked quickly from the broom closet where he had sat for the last hour. He stood outside Esther Goldstein's room and then turned and looked back at the central monitoring desk. He must hurry. The two aides were liable to come back any minute, and if they looked across the hall, they could see him through the cheap, pale blue curtains in Esther Goldstein's window. Either that, or they might check the EKG printouts and see that she was indeed "having a problem."

He moved inside and stared down at her sleeping figure. He had to do something about the oscilloscope. He looked at it, as her EKG reading bleeped across. On top of it was the warning squawk box with the volume knob. This would be easy—very easy indeed. He reached for the knob, turning it to the right, to the spot marked Off, smiling as he stared down at Esther. He twisted again, but it didn't seem to click off. He tried turning it again, but it was stuck. Christ . . . now what? He stared down at the knob, twisting it to the left, just to make sure.

Harry opened the door, groped around for the light, and banged his shin on something solid. A sharp pain shot up his leg and he cursed and reached down, this time banging his head.

"Shit," he said. "Shit. Come on, June, help me find the light."

"Here," she said. She turned it on and looked around. They were surrounded by old anesthesia machines, rubber tubing, ancient oxygen masks, and other paraphernalia no longer used by the hospital.

"Why don't they get rid of this junk?" June said, walking across the room. "It's just useless garbage."

Harry rubbed his head and gave her his best simian smile.

"It's not all useless," he said. "Look at this old table."

He walked to the end of the room, took some equipment off an old operating table, and jumped up.

80

"Turn off the light," he said, "and come over here."

"Harry," she said. "I don't know . . ."

But she was already walking toward the wall. The lights went out and Harry heard her coming toward him, bumping into things, cursing softly.

In the canteen, just ten feet down from the central monitoring desk, Rodgers and Hargrove, the two nurse's aides, sat having Cokes. Rodgers, a plain-looking girl with acne scars, sipped philosophically and stared down at the table. Hargrove, a very tall woman nicknamed Stilts, shook her head.

"I know just how it is," she said, "I know just how it is. All the bastards are alike. They say there was a sexual revolution. I say bullshit."

"You can say that again," said Sally Rodgers. "I mean it." She reached down in her tote bag and pulled out a half-pint of Jim Beam.

"We should be getting back," Stilts said.

"Ah, hell . . . I know, but June is handling it. Let's have one quick one, and . . ."

"Okay, you twisted my arm," Hargrove said. "But a quick one. Besides, I've got a special toast in mind."

"Right," Sally Rodgers said.

She ran her hand across her acne scars.

"Screw men," Hargrove said. "Screw 'em all."

"Amen," Sally said.

They drank with relish, then set down their cups.

"Back to the grind," Hargrove said.

Peter felt panicky. Jesus, the knob . . . He stared down at it. He couldn't tell if it was on or off. It seemed to be stuck. The oscilloscope still worked, but he had no idea what the volume was set at now that he had monkeyed

with it. He looked across the room, toward the nurses'
station. Maybe he should just leave. But no . . . he had
come this far . . .

He couldn't just quit. But there was no way to unplug
the damned thing. If you even tried to take it out of the
wall, the alarm would raise all hell in the nurses' station
. . . No, there was only one solution.

Quickly, he took out his nail clippers and opened up
the 'scope by removing the repair plate on the back. He
stuck his nail file into the Philips head screw on the
plate. There were four of them and he had to hurry. He
twisted and the screw turned, twisted again and again,
then the first one was in his pocket. Beneath him, Esther
Goldstein stirred . . . and he stopped and moved back
into the shadows. Then she settled down, and he was at
it again. The second came out more easily, and the third
and fourth seemed to fall out in his hands. He pulled off
the plate, looked inside at the maze of wires and springs,
and found the red wire which connected to the buzzer.
He reached in, tried pulling it out, but it put pressure on
the entire circuit. He had to be careful . . . If there was
anything that upset the EKG readings, he was through.

Suddenly there was a loud noise. But it was only
Esther snoring. There had to be another way to get to
that wire. He looked down at his nail clippers. There was
no choice. Swiftly, he edged them inside, being careful
not to touch any other part of the machinery. Then he
found the wire and clipped it cleanly. Finally, he re-
aligned the wire, just off center, so that from the outside
the plastic insulation seemed to match perfectly with
the other end, but inside the copper coils were no longer
in contact. Quickly, he picked up the repair plate and
began working with the screws. In a few minutes he had
all four of them back in. He checked the wall clock in
the nurses' station. Three fourteen—he had to hurry.

82

Then he looked down at Esther Goldstein, who was staring at him, wide awake.

"No, Harry. Oh, Christ, not up the ass. I can't stand it."

But he had her bent over now, bent over the old operating table, and he was taking his cock out of her cunt and starting to push it in her ass.

"It's going to be good, baby. You've just got to open yourself up to it. It's going to be very good."

"Oh, Harry, I don't know. Oh, God, all right. Give it to me now."

He thrust himself forward and she reached around and took his huge penis and began to rotate her ass and put it in. Harry felt as if he were going to explode. Oh, God, he needed this. And she had been good, very good, and she was being good now, taking it inch by inch and moaning.

"That's it, Harry. That's it . . . Give it to me. Right there. I waaaannnt it. Give it to me, Harry. I want you in there. Yes. Reach around and take my breasts. Now."

Harry reached and grabbed them. So damned large and hard and the nipples in between his fingers, and he was getting in deeper and deeper. But there was something just a little amiss. He hadn't been able to come yet. Christ, she had come three times but he hadn't made it yet. He kept thrusting at her, and she was wiggling harder now, taking his whole cock all the way in her and crying and rotating her ass. And Harry felt good, good, but not great. Christ, he was having trouble. Maybe all that doping, staying out late was finally getting to him. He was thirty-four. What was wrong with him?

"I want to take you in my mouth," she said. "I want you in my mouth."

Harry pulled out, turned and slid up on the seat. She

got down on her knees in front of him, opened her lips
and took his cock into her mouth. He felt as if he were
going to explode. He held her head and as she licked him
and sucked him, she frantically moved her head back
and forth. When Harry looked down she was masturbating herself with her left hand.

"Oh, Goooooooddd, Harry," she said, as she came up
for air. "Oh, Gooooooooddddd!"

"Christ," Harry said. "Not so loud, will you, June?"

As soon as he said it, he could feel himself go limp.
Oh shit . . . shit . . . he wasn't going to make it.

"Oh, Goooooooddddd, Harrrrrry," she cried again.

But now she was on the floor by herself, masturbating.
Harry felt like an anachronism. She didn't need him. A
robot would do just fine. He wished to hell she wouldn't
yell so loud. The bitch. He had to make it. He pulled her
up, grabbed her hair, and shoved her back on the operating table and shoved his cock inside her. She gave out
with a yell that could have been heard in the Bronx.

"Take it, bitch," Harry said. "Take every inch."

"We have got to get back," said Sally Rodgers. "We've
got to."

"I know," Hargrove said. "But I want to say one
thing. Men suck. They suck. After you get through all
your feminism, all your intellectual arguments, it comes
down to the old suck number."

"I know," Sally said. "Still, what are you gonna do?"

"I'm going to be gay," Hargrove said. "You ready for
that?"

Sally looked at her with huge eyes.

"We have to get back," she said.

"What are you doing there, young man?" Esther
said, staring up at him, wide awake.

84

"Sorry," Peter said, smiling, "I was just checking the monitor here. I didn't mean to waken you."

"Oh, that's all right," Esther said. "I was having a bad dream anyway."

"Really," Peter said. "Tell me about it."

"I was just dreaming of my husband...my late husband...I was having an argument with him."

Peter reached into his pocket, felt the syringe with the 500 units of insulin. He ran his fingers along the steel tip.

"What were you arguing about?" he said.

"Well...it wasn't exactly an argument. He was making me feel guilty for my life now. Oh, it's too late to go into it all. It's just that...this is all very depressing for me...just when you think you are starting to live, you get hit with something like this. Then you start to feel guilty...You know, 'Maybe I'm being punished for living this sort of life.' You know the feeling."

Peter smiled and pulled up a chair. He felt an infinite tenderness toward her.

"I do indeed," he said. "I know exactly what you mean."

"You're not just saying that?" Esther said, suspiciously.

"No, Esther," he said, "I am not just saying it."

"What's your name?"

"Peter," he said, "Dr. Peter Cross. I'm going to be your anesthesiologist."

"You mean I need surgery?" She began to get excited.

He reached toward her and took her hand.

"We're going to give you some tests in the morning. I'm going to be taking good care of you. You must trust me."

He spoke in a peaceful, reverential monotone, just like the Methodist ministers Lila Lee had taken him to hear before she got sick.

"I do," she said. "I don't know why I do . . . but I do. You seem to really care about me."

She smiled at him, and he squeezed her arm.

"I do care, Esther," he said. "I care very much. I have talked to your son, and I know what a special person you are."

"Barty?" she said. "He's such a square."

"But he loves you very much, Esther. He cares for you deeply. I don't think I've ever met a son who cared for his mother as much as he does you."

A tear came to her eye, and he felt her hand grip his forearm.

"I like you," she said. "And I'm sorry I'm crying . . . I am trying to be brave."

"You don't have to try in front of me, Esther," he said. "You don't have to be anything but yourself. I like you fine, just the way you are."

"I can't make it," Harry said. "I just can't get it off."

June Boswell was upside down, her legs wrapped around Harry's neck. Her neck was breaking from her own weight and she was exhausted, having come six times.

"We've got to get the hell back," she said. "I'm sorry, Harry. I really am, but we've got to get back."

Harry was livid.

"You're sorry?" he screamed. "You're fucking sorry? Shit."

Enraged, he looked down at her, her big breasts hanging down, her legs covered with sweat, and her crotch all moist and smelling of the East River, and he felt sick.

"Shit, June," he said.

Impulsively, violently, he took both her legs in his hand and flipped her over the table. She landed on her back on the floor.

86

"You bastard," she said. "You shitty male chauvinist bastard. I fucking hate you. You impotent ape."

She began to mimic a baboon, tickling her underarms and jumping about.

"Ummmga, ummmga," she said. "Ape can't make it."

Harry started to smash her, then he realized where he was and turned to find his pants.

"Asshole," she said, picking up her dress. "You'll be sorry, asshole."

"Yeah, right," Harry said, and he hit her in the face.

"So many of the doctors just don't care about the patients," Esther Goldstein said. "You know what I mean?"

"I do indeed," Peter said.

"I believe you," she said, patting his hand. "I really do. I wish you and Barty could be friends. You're strong. I can see that. He's such a weakling . . . and it's my fault."

"Nonsense," Peter said. "It's not your fault at all. You've done all you could."

"But I did too much," Esther said. "I made him a baby."

"No," Peter said, reaching for the needle. "He's a fine man. It's all right now. You've done fine. Now you deserve to be free."

She smiled as he stroked her arm and then her forehead.

"Yes," she said. "That's what I keep telling myself. But I still feel such guilt."

"No more," Peter said. "No more . . . From now on you will be free . . . free of all of it. Now, just relax . . . lie back . . . and shut your eyes. I'm going to give you something that will make you feel good. Really good. Okay?"

Esther Goldstein smiled.

"Okay," she said. "Sure . . . I like you, Dr. Cross . . ."

"Call me Peter," he said, sticking the syringe into her IV drip.

"Peter," she said, dozing, "you're my friend."

"Look," Sally said, "I don't want to hear about this, okay?"

"I'm having an identity crisis and you don't want to hear about it," Hargrove said. "That's fine. That's really fine."

She got out the bottle of Jim Beam again, but Sally got nervous and pushed her hand back down in the bag.

"Please," she said. "We've both got our exams coming up. I don't want to get thrown out. Now I'm going back down there."

"Don't worry," Hargrove said. "I just saw Yvonne heading that way."

Yvonne Neslogites walked down the hallway toward the central monitoring desk. She was a tall, thin woman with black hair and long, skinny legs. She felt she looked like an anorexic and often wore loose-fitting clothes so she might seem to possess a little more bulk. It seemed the crucial irony of her life that everyone in the world looked good thin but her. She merely looked runty, plucky at best. Like a cockney guttersnipe, a friend had once told her. Now she scraped along the hall, and got to the central monitoring station. She looked at her watch. Three twenty, only four more hours to go. She knew June would be glad to see her. She must be tired. But June wasn't there. No one was there. She looked over at the EKG readings . . . someone ought to keep up with those. Then she heard something in the hall behind her and she turned, sharply, in response.

She lay there in front of him, in perfect sleep. It had been so easy. Just hit her with the insulin, and she had fallen off into a coma, into a place beyond dreams. He felt the icy beauty of it throughout. Inside, the Space grew smaller. He felt solid, real . . . God, it was good . . . Her brain was gone, and very soon her heart would be his own. He stared down at her hand, caressed it. Then quietly, tenderly, he placed it over her heart.

Yvonne turned and saw June Boswell straggling up the hall toward the nurses' station. Her face was very, very red, and one of her hose was slightly twisted. From the other side of the hallway, she saw Rodgers and Hargrove coming back. What the hell was going on? She puts them in charge for a half hour and they screw up. Now she had to get the EKGs read . . . especially that new patient, Goldstein. She reached over in the tray and picked it up.

"Yvonne," June said, "I'm sorry."

Yvonne put the EKG printout down.

"What's wrong?"

"I got sick to the stomach. The flu . . . I don't know. I had to use the john."

"It's all right," Yvonne said. "I understand . . . but don't leave your post again. Really . . . if anything happened here . . ."

June buckled, and Hargrove and Rodgers caught her before she hit the floor.

Peter crouched by the door, watching the nurses. If they turned his way, he was done. Quickly he began to crawl down the hall toward the janitor's stairs. He had wanted to stay, to share it with Esther . . . She had triumphed . . . like Lorraine Bell . . . she had triumphed.

But he must move fast. He reached the door to the stairs, straightened up, and looked back at the nurses' station. All three of the nurses were huddled, talking to June.

As he made his way down the stairs to the first floor, he felt as though he were flying. And he blushed, nearly started to laugh, for no one else could see him hovering there, in the lobby of Eastern Medical, like some rare, fantastic bird of night.

12

Yvonne Neslogites stood in front of Dr. Beauregard's cluttered desk. Her left eyebrow twitched, and her palms were cold. In her hand she held a book, *How to Put on Pounds Sensibly*. She beat it against her skinny thigh and breathed in and out like a spluttering engine.

"Okay," Beauregard said, sitting coiled, his hands clasped in front of him in an effort to keep himself under control. "Let's go through this one more time. You tell me that you were in charge of the desk, but you left at ten of three to go help Dr. Thompson with a cut-down."

"That's right," Yvonne said. "He was having trouble finding a vein on Mrs. Martin. I had to help him with her."

"And when you left, June was in charge of the two aides, Jane Hargrove and Sally Rodgers."

"That's right."

"And?"

"They went on break at about two or three minutes before three... they went to the canteen to have a Coke. June was on her own. At approximately twelve after three she got sick and had to leave the desk. We all got back at the same time... about three twenty-six. I know because I happened to look at my watch then. June got back about three twenty-eight. She was weaving, almost fainting. We found Mrs. Goldstein at about quarter to four. When we checked the EKG...but if that buzzer—"

Beauregard nodded his head and cut her off.

"We'll get to that in a minute."

He punched his phone.

"Brigette. Send in Hargrove and Rodgers."

A second later the two aides came through the door. They looked as though they had seen a plane nose-dive onto the Long Island Expressway.

Jane Hargrove had large blue bags under her eyes. Sally Rodgers's skin looked like oatmeal. Both of them nodded to Yvonne and Beauregard and then dropped their eyes to the floor.

"All right," Beauregard said, "what happened?"

"I don't know," Jane Hargrove said. "I was on a break. I mean we were both on a break."

"That's right," Sally Rodgers said, "but we were only just down the hall. If June would have called us, we would have been right there. But I'll tell you what was even stranger . . ."

"What's that?" Beauregard said.

"The buzzer. It never went off."

"Maybe you just didn't hear it," Beauregard said. He stared at them hard. They both dropped their eyes as if on cue.

"Are you sure you were both in the canteen?" he said. "You didn't go anywhere else."

"No," they both said in unison.

Jane Hargrove ran her long fingers through her black hair. "We sat in the canteen the entire time. If the oscilloscope had gone off, we would have heard it."

"How about June?" Beauregard said. "Was she too sick to hear?"

Everyone was silent.

Beauregard pounded a huge fist on the table, scattering

his papers around the room. Sally Rodgers gasped.

"Look," he said, "I don't have time to play politics here. A patient has died. There is going to be a goddamned big deal made out of this. I don't like the looks of any of it . . . and if you two don't cooperate with me, you're through here. You understand. Now, what was wrong with June?"

The women exchanged nervous looks, and Beauregard sat straight up in his chair.

"She was sick," Jane Hargrove volunteered. "She was very sick. She said it just came over her . . . She felt she was going to faint . . ."

"Yes," Yvonne said. "She said . . . she fell in the ladies' room. She hit her head on the sink when she was trying to put some cold water on her face."

"Did you know that June was sick, Yvonne?"

"No."

Beauregard got up again and punched his fist into his open palm.

"She never mentioned she was sick at all?"

"No, Doctor, she didn't."

"Where is she now?"

"Home. She has the flu . . . I called her this morning. She had to go see Dr. Chapman."

"That's very strange," Beauregard said. "Very weird . . . Everybody leaves, and nobody hears the buzzer."

"But I'm telling you," Hargrove said. "If that buzzer had gone off, we would have heard it. You know how loud those things are. We checked the 'scope and it was on."

Beauregard punched his phone again.

"Brigette, send in Jimmy Myers."

Beauregard waited, tapping a pencil on his fingers. The door opened and a monstrous man weighing three hundred pounds came waddling into the room. He wore size forty-six chinos with huge tool pockets which seemed to hang down to his ankles. Hammers, screwdrivers, saws, and wiring hung off him. He looked like a junk sculpture. His hair stood out like spokes and his cheeks were blotched red. In his chubby pink fingers were two Hostess Twinkies.

"Hi ya, Doc," Jimmy Myers said.

He turned and bowed to the nurses.

"Madams," he said.

"Jimmy," Beauregard said, "I want you to look over the oscilloscope that was in Esther Goldstein's room, the woman who died of a heart attack, Number Six on Coronary Care."

"Right, Doc. What's the problem?"

"It didn't go off last night. I want you to determine what happened to it."

Jimmy Myers stuck an entire Twinkie into his mouth. He looked over at Yvonne's book, took it out of her hand, smearing icing across the cover.

"Just what I need," he said. "Sensible pounds . . . most of the ones I've got are downright crazy. I get me a couple of them sensible pounds, I'll be a more well-rounded person."

He gave a tremendous horselaugh and nudged Yvonne in her skinny ribs.

"Well-rounded, git it?" he said.

Then he turned around and waddled out the door, dropping his Twinkie wrapper in Jane Hargrove's lap.

"Jesus," Jane said.

"Yeah," Beauregard said, "he's a little weird, but he's a very good technician. If there was anything wrong with that machine, he'll find it. And if there wasn't, he'll find that too."

Beauregard gazed intensely at the three women and all of them dropped their eyes.

94

13

He stood in June Boswell's living room in Chelsea. In front of him was a Delisciosca Monstera, a huge green plant that crawled up a trellis toward the shaft of sunlight that found its way through the barred back window. June Boswell sat on the couch, still dressed in her bathrobe and pajamas. Her face was red and she had a bottle of tetracycline sitting on the coffee table. He noticed the date—February 1—yesterday.

"I'm sorry you're feeling bad, June," Beauregard said. "You feel any better?"

"No," June said. "Dr. Chapman thinks it's that flu that's going around."

"Yeah," Beauregard said, fingering the plant and staring around at the plastic coffee table, the homemade bookshelves. Suddenly the place reminded him of Heather—their good days together at Georgetown.

"That bruise on your head..." Beauregard said. "It must have been a nasty fall."

June looked squarely at him and shook her head.

"It was," she said. "I just got violently ill...That's why I've been a little scared to come back to work. Look, Dr. Beauregard, I know this is causing you a lot of trouble at the hospital, and I feel terrible about it."

"About what?" Beauregard said.

"I don't follow you," June said.

"About the trouble it's causing me—and you—or about Esther Goldstein."

"Well, of course, I feel sick about her. She was such a nice lady. Are you kidding—I couldn't sleep last night, and that was after two sleeping pills. I just couldn't believe it."

"You know you could be suspended for something like this, June."

June Boswell nodded her head.

"I know it . . . but look . . . I got sick . . . violently sick."

"And at no time when you were in the ladies' room did you hear the oscilloscope go off?"

"It never went off," June said. "I'm sure of that. The john is only fifteen feet away. I'm sure I would have heard it."

Beauregard nodded and managed a smile.

"Listen," he said, "I believe you . . . but this could get rough. The Medical Examiner is doing an autopsy on Esther Goldstein today, and her son is very, very excited. He's calling for your resignation, as are a number of other people. Naturally, since you are a good nurse, I want to protect you. But I've got to know everything. Is there anything you've forgotten?"

June sighed, leaned back on the gilt-edged pillow, and shook her head.

"No," she said, "that's it. I just got sick at three ten or so . . . went in there for ten minutes . . . and when I got back, she was gone . . . I mean it was about ten till four before we picked it up on her EKG . . . that goddamned buzzer . . . It's all a nightmare."

Suddenly she started to cry, and Beauregard went over to her and put his arm around her. She put her face on his arm, then drew back. He noticed a red blotch on her cheek . . . slightly raw and discolored. He hadn't seen that before.

"Your cheek," he said.

"I know," she said quickly, "it looks horrible. I hit my face on the floor . . . after I bounced off the sink. God . . . I'm so sorry."

Beauregard nodded and patted her arm.

"I'll be in touch," he said. He patted her arm again, then let himself out.

14

She felt the coolness of his hand as it grasped her own.
She wondered if it was a little clammy because he was
nervous. Certainly he seemed that way, off center, a bit
out of sorts. On the other hand, he seemed to be enjoying their walk through the park. Now, in the Sheep
Meadow, they watched another couple walk across the
frozen grass, their big black-and-tan Airedale in front of
them. The couple stopped and hugged one another, then
kissed, and Debby was surprised to feel Peter's grip
tighten. She turned to him, staring up into his dark eyes.

"You look very handsome," she said.

"No," he said, holding her. "I'm not even fit company
for anyone as beautiful as you."

"That's simply not so," she said. "I don't know what
your mother did to you, but whatever it was, you should
really forget it... you're not a gangly little kid any
more. This isn't Baltimore, and you're not the odd kid
out. You're with me... In Central Park... New York
City... and I might add that I'm crazy about you."

He frowned a little and blushed. She kissed him on the
cheek and hugged him fiercely.

"What's wrong?" she said, staring into his eyes.

"Nothing," he said. "Only I'm a little embarrassed I
told you all those things about myself... I've never told

them to anyone before."

"But that's the point," she said. "You have to talk about them . . . deal with them . . . then they'll go away."

He smiled and put his arm around her, took the bag out of his coat, and tossed some peanuts to the squirrels.

"Just like that, huh?" he said.

"No, of course not. Not just like that . . . But it's a start."

"Yes," he said. "Sure . . ."

But he didn't sound convinced.

They crossed the path, moving through the herd of joggers coming toward them.

"Out for their health fix," Peter said as they walked into the hilly wooded area just above Wollman Skating Rink.

"What's wrong with jogging?" Debby said.

Again he gave that curious, imperial smile, as if he were onto something she would never fathom. Though she loved him, it did irritate her.

"Just that jogging seems such a petty way to spend one's time. Do you know what I mean?"

She smiled at him, now open and friendly, and he shrank back a little, his face lost in the gray shadows.

"No," she said, "I don't see it like that . . . I mean, I don't do it personally, but I know it's good for you."

"Good for you?" he said.

"Yes," she said. "It's good for the heart, for your pulse, your wind, keeps you toned up."

He reached for her and held her to him again, and kissed her on the nose.

"Of course it is," Peter said. "I'm just being cranky. I know that . . . but I've got my own brand of medicine."

"What?" she said.

"You," he said, then he kissed her on the mouth.

She felt his long, strong arms, sinewy, tight-muscled.

She was always surprised by their strength. He wasn't muscular. But he was surprisingly strong.

"You are really corny," she said, smiling and holding onto him so he would realize that she loved it.

He smiled again, and they walked arm in arm down the steps toward the shouting children with their flashing skates hanging over their shoulders. They walked up to the top of the rink and looked down on the skaters—hundreds of them, wearing bright red and blue and orange sweaters, trailing brilliant scarves.

"Aren't they beautiful?" Debby said.

"Yes, they are," Peter said. "They are beautiful."

He looked away toward the branches of the winter trees.

She smiled and held him again. He had seemed so happy lately, so relaxed. He had even been sleeping well . . . not like the bad weeks last month. Now she could feel his back muscles—relaxed, and she thought, He is learning to be at ease with himself . . . He's learning and I'm helping him. Then she became afraid. Things happened so fast in New York. She had promised herself she would give herself time . . . play the field a little. But that had only been a fantasy, for at heart she was still a country girl. She had the new wardrobe, the new facial, and her hair done at Bonwit Teller, but one couldn't change what was inside so easily. She was basically small-town and serious . . . and he was unlike any man she had ever met. And now he was beginning to fall in love. He hadn't said it yet, but she knew. She clung to him, and he looked down at her and smiled, then kissed her forehead. Beneath them the flashing skates cut through the ice.

They entered the revolving doors to the Woodward Hotel on West 55th Street.

She led him through a narrow hallway to the dark, L-shaped room in the back of the lobby. A Japanese man with a long scar on his cheek smoked from a golden cigarette holder. He stared blankly at them, then bowed and led them to their stools at the counter.

"Enjoy your meal," the man said.

Debby took Peter's arm and he managed a smile.

"This is fun," she said. "I've always wanted to eat at a sushi bar."

Behind the counter a young man picked up a long, gleaming knife and pointed at the raw fish in the glass case.

"Squid," Debby said. "That looks wonderful."

Peter smiled and stared at the pink meat, at the tiny suction cups.

"Wonderful?" he said. "That's hard to believe."

He laughed in spite of himself. She made him feel good. Then he drew back.

The man behind the counter wiped the long, glinting knife off with a towel. Peter stared at the blade, transfixed.

"I think I'll have the *Nori Chozube*," Debby said to him.

She smiled at Peter and pointed it out on the menu.

"That's the seaweed and rice. And I'll also have the *Sake Chozuke* . . . that's the salted salmon on rice."

The man started to cut with the knife, slicing through the meat deftly, quickly . . . like a surgeon. Peter saw Esther Goldstein sitting in front of him, and suddenly he began to sweat. His arms tingled and his hands were absolutely cold. He felt the Space moving inside of him, calling to him. His mouth was dry and he felt the air leaving his stomach.

"Excuse me a minute," he said.

Quickly, he got up, headed back through the restaurant, and suddenly came upon the Japanese with the golden holder. The man smiled at him, flashing a golden tooth, and Peter felt his knees buckle. He grabbed the man's arm.

"The bathroom," he said. Now the entire room was swirling about, and he felt as if he were going to cry out. Then from behind there was a hand on his back, steadying him. When he turned, it was Debby. Seeing her intensified his emotions. He was out of his depth, felt as though he were going to crash to the rug.

"Let me alone," he said. "I've just got to get to the men's room. Let me alone . . . I'll be fine."

He was barely aware of the words. Debby seemed to be talking to him from the far end of binoculars. He turned and followed the golden cigarette holder which pointed down a short corridor toward the men's room. Once inside, he went into the stall and held onto the walls. The toilet bowl below him was spotless, white, white like the tiles of the OR. He stared down at it and felt as though he could fall into the water. He ripped a piece of toilet paper off the roll and wiped the spittle from his mouth, folded it over and wiped off his eyes. He took a deep breath, came out of the stall, splashed some water on his face, and went back out.

"Peter," Debby said, waving to him from a booth, "are you all right?"

"Yes," he said, smiling a little. "I'm fine now."

"What was it?"

She put her hand on his arm, and he wanted to take it off, but he didn't dare.

"Nothing . . . nothing at all. I guess just seeing that squid. I've never eaten raw fish like this before."

"Well, you don't have to get raw fish," she said. "They have trout and blue point oysters, and lots of traditional seafood."

102

"No, that's fine," he said. "I'll have some of the cod-fish. What's it called?"

"*Tarako Chazuke*," she said. "Though I'm probably not even close with the pronunciation. You sure you're all right?"

"Sure," Peter said. "Well, to tell you the truth, I guess I was thinking about work. I still keep thinking about that death in the cardiac care ward. You'd think I'd forget about it by now—but then seeing that raw meat . . . I don't know . . ."

Debby nodded and patted his cheek.

"I know exactly what you mean. Dr. Beauregard has been crazy these last few weeks. It's awful. And poor June. I think they're being a little rough on her . . . she couldn't help it if she got sick."

"No . . . I understand the Medical Examiner has the case."

"Had the case," Debby said. "I was in Dr. Beauregard's office just this morning, and I saw the ME report. Death due to heart attack. They say the buzzer on the oscilloscope was stuck."

"Yes," Peter said. "That is really weird. So coincidental."

Debby smiled and threw up her hands.

"Our lives are so crazy," she said.

Now Peter ran his index finger around his collar.

"What were you doing with . . . I mean in Beauregard's office?" he said, trying to sound casual.

"Oh, he asked me in," Debby said.

"Why?" Peter said.

"Oh, he just wanted to ask us over for dinner," Debby said.

"What?" Peter said, excited.

"Yes," Debby said. "I've meant to tell you all day. His wife is home now and he said that he wants us to meet her. He really likes you. He said he thought you were a very interesting young man."

Peter felt the anxiety shooting over him again. He blinked, took a deep breath. Suddenly he was surrounded by people he cared about . . . now that he had become himself . . . but what if they knew . . . what if any of them even suspected?

"We don't have to go, Peter," Debby said, as the waiter brought them their dishes.

Peter stared down at the raw fish. Quickly he put some of the hot green mustard and the soy sauce on his plate, mixed them together, then cut off some of the cod, and picked it up with his chopsticks.

"No," he said. "I like Dr. Beauregard too. I wouldn't miss his dinner party for the world."

He was surprised at how well he was able to use the chopsticks. It was as if he had been doing it all his life.

104

15

"Peter and Debby, I'd like you to meet my wife, Heather," Beauregard said.

Peter exchanged glances with Debby and shook Heather Beauregard's firm hand. He looked at her long model's face—the perfect cheekbones, the skin like velvet, the green eyes, and blond hair cut a little longer than Debby's, but just as full and silky down her back. Cross found looking at her disconcerting. It was like meeting a movie star close up. She was too good-looking, really . . . like a vision. And her body. Cross tried not to look at it. She was so obviously a physical person, her tight Halston gown, which trailed to the floor, her long, thin, but strong legs. Peter smiled but dropped his eyes.

"It's really a pleasure to meet you," Heather said in a low, throaty voice. "Beau has told me so much about you . . . and I mean that. Actually, I don't know whether it's to your advantage or not, because when my husband likes someone, he expects them to be as totally devoted to their work as he is. Which means you'll sleep once a month and have no time for Debby."

Debby and Peter laughed as Heather shook Debby's hand, but Beauregard protested.

"Not true," he said. "That is simply not true. I'm starting a new regime. Tonight. The hospital is going to

have to share equal billing with my family and friends
... I mean it.”

He poured each of them a glass of champagne and
lifted his glass.

“A toast,” he said, “to friendship and to the return of
my lovely wife, who graces this room.”

“Hear, hear,” Debby said.

They clicked their glasses and drank the champagne.
Peter loved the taste of it . . . but then felt a swirling
sensation in his stomach. He was being bought . . . bought
off with all this . . . friendship, luxury. He looked around
the room, at the modern paintings, at the white carpet,
the mirrored walls, the fireplace with the wrought iron,
at the plants, the elegant bar with its leather-covered bar
stools, and from the living room through the French
doors out into the dining room, where the maid put the
finishing touches on the long, beautiful dinner table.
This was “the class” his father had resented so desperately, had dreamed of, and finally had killed himself
over.

“Well,” Heather said, “come here, Peter. There is
someone special I want you to meet.”

She took him by the hand and led him around the
corner, to the bedroom, and he felt the sweat breaking
out on his brow. There was an old English door with
stained-glass windows, and when they opened it, he stared
in on a beautiful little girl, as fair-haired and perfectly
complexioned as her mother.

“Sarah, I want you to meet Peter Cross.”

“Hello,” Sarah said, sitting on her bed, holding a copy
of Catch 22 in her hands. She wore a pink pullover and
tight Levis, and her eyes were as intense as any Peter
had ever seen. He couldn’t believe she was only twelve.

“Peter is the best anesthesiologist at Eastern,” Heather
said, patting him on the back. “So you be nice to him . . .

106

or he'll put you under."

Sarah giggled and reached out her hand. Peter stepped forward and shook it.

"Weird," Sarah said. "What a weird job. Putting people under."

Peter felt as though he were stung. Then he got hold of himself.

"Not really," he said. "It's my job to prevent pain. When you think of it that way, it's natural as ... eating or sleeping."

"Still," Sarah said, "it's scary."

She smiled so good-naturedly that Peter felt all right. He shouldn't let a child upset him anyway. Except she didn't look like a child ... her body was just starting to develop, and her grace was that of a mature woman. It was unnerving. Behind him, he heard Beauregard talking with Debby.

"Come meet my precocious daughter," he said.

Then they were all in the room, and Debby and Sarah were smiling at one another, shaking hands. Peter looked at them, then at Heather and Beauregard, dressed casually in his Ralph Lauren tweed pants, his herringbone shirt and English tweed jacket. Though Debby was from upstate, no one who walked in here would ever know it. They all belonged here ... by virtue of their looks, their ease with one another. He was an imposter. The thought made him feel like bolting. But he smiled affably, and soon they were back in the living room, smiling at one another and drinking more champagne. Within minutes Peter felt giddy, and with the giddiness felt an *esprit de corps* that melted his fear.

"Well, Paris is wonderful," Heather was saying to Debby, "especially wonderful when you are young and in love. If Beau ever gives you two any time off, I insist that you go. I have a poet friend who has a house over there . . . and he just got a scholarship to teach in Montana . . . the French are crazy about the Wild West . . . anyway, he'd probably rent you the place for practically nothing. Oh, you really should go."

Debby sat down next to Peter on the white couch. She touched his knee.

"Did you hear that?" she said. "God, I'd love to go to Paris, wouldn't you, Peter?"

"Yes . . . of course," Peter said.

The way the light hit the room . . . the way it came in off 61st Street. Even the light in the room looked expensive and successful. Peter thought of his own barren place on West 12th. He felt as if he were a starving man who was being offered overly rich food.

"The life is so wonderful there," Heather said. "People take time with things. I'll tell you . . . I got off the plane the other day and the first thing I noticed was the stress factor here. People wear their stress on their faces. You can actually see the difference."

Beauregard smiled and poured everyone another round of champagne.

"That's true," Beauregard said. "I remember when we went to Sweden the first time . . . I got back here and it was like entering the depressive ward of the hospital. You simply can't notice it unless you've been. How's everyone doing?"

Peter and Debby smiled. Peter was doing fine; in fact, he had never felt more lightheaded, more carefree. He looked up and there was the maid staring at him. In her hand was a silver tray on which were twenty or thirty hors d'oeuvres.

"This is terrific," he said. He took one and put it in his mouth. It was warm and full of a delicious cheese. He sat back and stared at Debby, and again noted how well she seemed to go with the company, the decor. As if she

108

were meant for such a life. He felt a rumbling in his stomach, but he drank some more champagne and it quieted down.

"Speaking of stress," Peter said, "I think maybe this champagne might be better than all the tranquilizers in the world."

"Well, have some more," Heather said, and before Peter could protest, she was pouring for him. He sipped and sat back, and Heather began telling them about all the places she'd been in the last year. London, Belgium, Germany...

"Oh," Debby said, "we simply have to go, Peter. Wouldn't it be wonderful?"

"Yes," Peter said, "I'd really love that."

He was surprised at himself for saying so. Indeed, up until very recently he hadn't wanted to leave his room. Now here he was chatting with these sophisticated people and holding his own. He felt strange, like he was swimming in unfamiliar waters... but such pleasant waters. They seemed to hold him up effortlessly.

"How long will you be staying now that you're back?" he heard himself ask. Immediately, he knew he had committed a faux pas.

"Well," Heather said, "I'm not certain. I'm supposed to help a friend who is opening a bookstore in Montmartre... I did promise to go back for that... in a month."

Beauregard cleared his throat and smiled a little painfully at Peter.

"I didn't mean..."

But Beauregard raised his hand.

"It's perfectly all right," he said, "but we're betting that Heather won't leave at all. I think we've got a few magic tricks to keep her here."

"Keep feeding me these hors d'oeuvres," Heather said.

"And this champagne."

"There is a basement of it," Beauregard said.

"You're kidding," Debby said. "You've got a wine cellar?"

"Well," Beauregard said, "not exactly a cellar. More like a wine room. Temperature-controlled. Just right. I'll show you after dinner."

"Speaking of which," called Mrs. O'Shea from the other room, "dinner is served."

She rang a golden gong, and Debby and Peter laughed. As they walked into the dining room, Debby pinched Peter's ass.

He turned and smiled at her.

"Are you really interested in books?" Peter said, as Mrs. O'Shea served them their seafood salads.

"Oh, yes, very much so . . . and I hear you are a great admirer of Poe."

"That's right," Peter said.

He reached across the table and saw Sarah there. Her perfect face . . . the kind of girl he dreamed of as a child. The champagne had made him feel as though he were floating, as though anything were possible. He could not look at her, though. She was so physical . . . It was unnatural in a child. He wished to God they hadn't seated him next to her.

"You know," Heather said, "the French are crazy about Poe."

"Yes?" Peter said. "They are?"

"Certainly," Heather said. "Baudelaire really discovered him."

Peter shook his head as he ate his salad.

"Of course," he said, "men of talent are rarely appreciated in this culture."

"Oh, I don't know that that's true," said Beauregard.

110

"That's the argument I hear all the time. But you take our field. In spite of all the backbiting and infighting, I think as a whole the medical profession in this country, and in anesthesiology in particular, is open now to experimentation."

Peter thought of the men who discovered the first anesthetics . . . Horace Wells, who had been laughed into madness . . .

"No," he said, "that's not true. It's true with you . . . Because you set up an atmosphere at Eastern that encourages experimentation. But it's certainly not the rule. The safe ways—the tried-and-true—are the only things most of the administrators want to use."

"I'd have to agree with Peter, Beau," Heather said.

Beauregard nodded and smiled, as if he agreed.

Encouraged, Peter went on.

"And as for Poe," he said, sipping the champagne again, "you know, I think few people really understand what he was up to. He was a visionary . . . His tales weren't just horror tales meant to shock, but explorations into dreams, into moments of pure consciousness."

Heather leaned over the table now and nodded enthusiastically. "That's right," she said. "He was trying to get outside of what is known . . . altogether . . . the French poets were the same way . . . what was it Rimbaud said, about the systematic derangement of all the senses . . . that's what Poe was after. He was a revolutionary . . . and this damned country was too conservative, too puritanical to understand a thing he was doing."

Peter felt thrilled. He couldn't have put it better himself. Heather Beauregard was almost too good to believe. Not only beautiful but excited by ideas. He felt as though she would understand him.

"Well," Beauregard said, "excuse me for playing devil's advocate, but my feeling about 'systematic derangement' and all that stuff is it's pretty scary. I remember the 60's when kids were talking like that... though I would scarcely blame poor Edgar Allan Poe for it. Anyway, they were all popping drugs, psychedelics, and the like, in an effort to become instant visionaries, and a lot of them are now thirty-year-old cripples with half a brain."

Debby held up her glass and nodded.

"I'll have to go with that," she said. "Whatever happened to good old-fashioned love and friendship. I don't know, maybe I'm just an uptight Yankee, but it seems to me there are certain roots..."

Everyone chuckled around the table, including Peter, who was again amazed at how pleasant he felt. It was almost as if he had wings and had been lifted, magically, out of the ordinary and dull into a dream world where all the visions were full of bright yellow light. Perhaps this was success... this was what it meant all along. To be with brilliant people... to talk and be friends with them... and even in disagreement to realize their essential worth. But he felt vaguely suspicious... It seemed to be too good to be true. Certainly it was totally different from anything he had experienced before... but, Christ, it felt good.

"Well, a toast," Beauregard said, holding up the wine glasses. "I propose a toast to Peter and Debby... the good young people on our staff... and good friends..."

Peter smiled and found himself joyously clinking glasses with the others. Heather smiled at him, Debby put her hand on his leg under the table, and Beauregard looked down on him calmly, full of pride... like a father beaming at the All American son.

"Oh, Lord," Beauregard said. "We've run out of wine."

He held up the empty bottle and turned it over. Mrs. O'Shea was by his side.

"Yes," Beauregard said. "We could use a little more...

112

but maybe this is a good time to show Peter the wine room. How about it, Dr. Cross?"

"Sure," Peter said.

Again he felt that excitement. Like a kid going down at Christmas to get his train set. He felt foolish but too damned good to care.

They descended the spiral staircase into the basement, and at the bottom came to a dark oak door. Beauregard pushed it open, and Peter was amazed at the coolness of the room. It was at least ten degrees cooler than upstairs.

'Brr," he said.

"Yes, it's always fifty degrees in here," Beauregard said. "And here we have the wine."

He gestured toward the wine bins, and Peter stared at the many bottles with their silver and golden seals. Beauregard walked over to one of the bins.

"Here we have a fine Bordeaux," he said. "Château Mouton Rothschild, 1959. It's really full-bodied, well-developed . . . and, as they say, has a beautiful nose."

He handed the bottle to Peter, who took it awkwardly, afraid he would drop it. Wine cellars were, to him, the stuff of movies or TV.

"And here," Beauregard said, moving down the line, "we have a Château Lafite, 1961. Though '59 is slightly better, this is also very, very good."

Peter took the bottle in his hand, and this time a strange sensation came over him. It was as though the wine was more than simply a liquor to drink. It seemed to possess the qualities of a talisman, magic to stave off the ordinariness of life. Suddenly he understood how serious wine tasters felt . . . wine—collecting it, making it, tasting it—was a way of life, an aristocracy of the senses . . . and he felt delighted, sophisticated.

Beauregard smiled and pulled out another bottle.

"Here we go," he said. "One of my personal favorites

...a Château Latour, 1964. They say the '59 is better, but I love the taste of this one. Perhaps we should take this one upstairs..."

Peter nodded, and Beauregard handed him the bottle, but suddenly there was a call from up above.

"Beau?"

It was Heather.

"Yes?"

"There is someone here to see you. He says it's important."

Beauregard smiled at Peter and shrugged. "Even tonight," he said, patting Peter's arm. "I wanted to show you the rest of the place...but why don't you look around on your own. I'll see you in a few minutes."

Peter held the wine in his hands.

"Sure, Beau," he said.

Beauregard smiled and left the room, and Peter heard his footsteps as he went up the steps.

He stood in the cool, dark room, trying to enjoy it as he had a minute ago, but something had changed. It didn't seem as wonderful as when Beauregard had been there. No, it was empty without Beauregard...almost as if the room itself responded to the real aristocrat, but as soon as he left, the room knew that Peter was a fake. He began to feel uncomfortable; he put the wine back in its rack and went up the steps.

Then he saw Jimmy Myers walk by the kitchen door. He ducked back, felt the sweat on his neck. Jimmy Myers...the oscilloscope...he saw himself cutting the wires...He took a deep breath and finished climbing the steps to the kitchen. He looked into the room. No one there. Then he heard footsteps from the hallway and heard Mrs. O'Shea. He ducked back onto the top step, heard her walk by him, open the refrigerator, get something, then head back to the dining room. He entered the

114

kitchen, saw a hallway to the left. He slid close to the wall and came upon a half-open door.

"You're sure," Beauregard said.

"Absolutely, Doc," Jimmy said.

"Christ, Jimmy, don't spill your Ho Ho's all over the rug. Mrs. O'Shea will throw a fit."

"Sorry, Doc. But that's the lowdown. I checked the switch. It was broken all right, but the way it was broken showed it was still off. So there is no reason for anybody to tamper with the wires inside."

"Unless," Beauregard said, "they weren't sure the switch was off, and the only way they could really be sure was to clip the wires. But that's crazy. You know what you're saying?"

"Yeah, Doc. I know exactly what I'm saying. Look, I've seen wires that wore out before. First of all, they get a kind of corroded look . . . you know, they are just too old. Well, this wire was new. Do you understand? There was no way for it to wear out. And what's more, it was clipped. You don't have to be an electronics expert to tell the difference between a clipped wire and a beat-up one. That's just the way it is."

"Yeah," Beauregard said, "I understand that. But isn't it perfectly possible that the wire was put in broken. You said yourself that it was off center . . . almost touching but not quite. So who's to say that the wire wasn't that way when we put it in. It was just a lemon."

"The same thing occurred to me, Doc. Two days ago I had that bum Calvin testing these things out. He was supposed to go over every one of them, since we had that trouble with the 'scope on the ninth floor."

"So—did he check?"

"Well—I can't reach him. His old lady says he's out." Jimmy laughed around the wad of gum in his mouth. "Out my ass—he's probably too scared to come to the phone. Anyway, tomorrow is payday—he'll be in—I can get the story then."

"Seems to me if he tested it, he'd have picked up on the stuck knob." Beau was frankly glad to have Calvin to blame instead of his staff. "I bet he never checked the damn thing and we lost a patient—there's going to be lots of trouble, Jimmy. I'm not losing one of my best nurses because your assistant was too stoned or too stupid to do what you told him to."

Jimmy stopped chomping and was silent, wrapping his mind around the implications of what would happen when he nailed down Calvin.

There was a silence, and Peter breathed a little better. There was nothing Myers could say to that.

"I don't know, Doc," Jimmy said. "This kind of thing happens, but the wires, that seems mighty strange to me. You might find one oscilloscope with one bad wire, but one with a bad wire and a bad switch . . . that's almost impossible."

Again there was a silence. Then Peter heard movement in the kitchen and quickly ducked into the bathroom. He locked himself in and stared at his face in the mirror. Amazing how relaxed he looked, how together. He knew the rest of the dinner was going to be anything but calm.

"Peter, you're acting extremely childish."

He looked down at her as they rode up Second Avenue. There were tears in her eyes, and he wanted to stop and hold her, but there was no way. He had been so damned happy . . . so ecstatic . . . He had thought for a while . . . Christ, it was pathetic really . . . thought that he was like everybody else—make clever conversation, enjoy the good food, drink good wine, be successful . . . but it wasn't true. He was marked out now, changed utterly by what he had done. They were moving toward him, get-

116

ting ready to nail him . . . Oh, they still acted friendly, still patted him on the back, but soon, soon they would start to hunt . . . unless he stopped completely . . . but there was no way to do that . . . He had the Space to answer to . . . and he was taking it out on her. He didn't want to . . . He really didn't . . . but he couldn't help it . . .

"I got so sick of it all," he said. "The fancy conversation, the fucking talk about Paris and Germany, the goddamned wine cellar. It was all so Upper East Side la-di-dah, and if that wasn't bad enough, you seemed to be taken in by it."

He pounded his hands on the steering wheel.

"But I don't understand," she said. "What you're saying just doesn't make sense. You seemed to be having fun too . . . until . . . I don't know . . . until you came back from the wine cellar. Did you and Beau have a disagreement?"

"Beau?" he said. "It's 'Beau,' is it? I love that . . . I really do. We go over there one night and you start calling him fucking Beau. It makes me sick. It really does. You were so sucked in by all that slick shit. I can't believe it."

"But he's your friend. Come on, Peter. Tell me what happened between you. What is it?"

She tried to reach for him, but he smacked her hand away.

"You were flirting with him," he said, surprising himself with the absurd allegation. "You like him, don't you? Maybe you'd like to sleep with him . . . huh? You've had the lackey . . . Maybe you'd like to make it with the suave, debonair rich boss?"

"Peter?"

She began to cry for real now, and he looked out the window at miserable, corroding Second Avenue and it seemed the perfect reflection of his soul. How they had tricked him ... Letting him have a taste of it and then pulling it all out from under him ... He would never be safe ... never ... and never be taken in again.

"Peter," she said, as they pulled up to her apartment, "I'm sorry you feel this way, but I never flirted with Dr. Beauregard. I just want you to know ... that I love you. I do. I don't like to see you like this. I feel like there is something wrong ... something you're not telling me ... that's making you take off at me like this."

"No," he said, "there isn't anything. I'm just disgusted with myself for going along with all that crummy, phony, charming crap ... and with you, too."

She looked over at him, and the sight of her eyes and long blond hair pierced him; he felt it all the way to the bone.

"Peter," she said, reaching over again. But he slapped her hand hard, and she got out of the car and ran up to the apartment house, crying.

He gunned the motor, tires squealing as he headed up the long, dark block.

16

Dios paced nervously up and down his office. He picked up the statue of the Su God that he kept with him at all times. The things he had been through with it. He felt dislocated, nervous, and when the door opened behind him, he jumped, nearly dropping the statue on the floor.

"Hey, pardner," Harry Gardner said, "calm down."

"Yeah," Dios said, "calm down. You're right, Harry. The truth of the matter is, I'm the one should be calm—you nervous."

"Why's that?" Harry said, sittting in the rocker across from Dios's desk.

"They are gonna hang you if they find out," Dios said.

"Find out what?" Harry said.

"Oh, come on, Harry," Dios said. "At least three of the nurses I know say they saw you with June Boswell the night that lady died in CCU."

"When?" Harry said. He walked toward Dios and snorted out his breath.

Dios reached into his desk drawer, pulled out a bottle of Rémy Martin, and poured them both a drink.

"What's the story?" Harry said, accepting the glass from Dios.

"You should be tense because a couple of the nurses

have been talking about you and June Boswell. There's a rumor going around that you were with her. Though I don't think it's gotten back to Beauregard yet."

"That's a lie," Harry said. But he drank the cognac quickly, then he wiped his mouth with the back of his hand, and drew in a deep breath.

"Is it?" Dios said. "Tell me the truth, Harry. Were you with her that night—getting a little?" Dios liked to use these Yankee phrases. So descriptive.

"No," Harry said. "Hey, what is this—the Spanish Inquisition?"

"No, Harry," Dios said. "Just some talk among friends." Harry walked over to the desk, cracking his knuckles. "Nervous, Harry?"

"No . . . well, yeah . . . You're making me nervous. Hey, you're the one who got all hot about Cross after that gomer died. I think you're a goddamn paranoid—I think you got a thing about anesthesiologists." Harry was trying to keep it light, but he sipped steadily at the drink.

"I don't like Peter," Dios said, running his hand over his huge ivory face. "I don't like him, but he wasn't seen up there, Harry; you were."

"Yeah? Well, so maybe I was up there—and visiting June—so what?"

"Maybe you visited her for a while, then walked in and greased that Goldstein lady."

Harry looked down at Dios and then reached across the desk and grabbed him by the lapels.

"Listen, you asshole, I don't want to hear any more of this shit, you hear me. Or your ass will be back cutting sugarcane. You get me?"

He pushed Dios back hard in the chair and started out the door.

"I'd be careful," Dios said in a monotone. "If I was you, Harry, I'd look out for my ass."

120

"Hello, June?"

"Harry . . . Harry . . . I'm afraid."

"It's all right, baby. It's all right. I've been keeping it cool for you. You aren't going to get suspended. It's okay."

"I've got to face the board, Harry. They are going to be rough, Harry. They are going to ask me a lot of questions . . . you know that? Like what kind of sickness did I have?"

"You tell them you had the flu."

"Why didn't I tell them before?"

"It came on sudden. The stomach virus. It's happening all over the Big Apple. No sweat."

"But it's not going to be easy, Harry. Beauregard was back over here. He questioned me again. There's a problem. They talked to Yvonne again and asked her what hallway I was coming down when she saw me, and she said the north hall."

"So?"

"Harry, the women's room is on the south hall. What was I doing on the north hall? Harry . . . can you come over?"

"Ah, not right now, Junie. Got some work. But I'll call tomorrow. I love you, June."

"I love you, Harry."

Harry hung up and turned to the tall girl with the black hair who was waiting for him at the bar.

"Back from the dead," he said, smiling at her.

"Oh, Harry," she said, "you're such a card."

Beauregard sat in his office holding the wire, while in front of him Jimmy Myers worked on his Tasty Pie.

"I don't know," Beauregard said. "Now that you've looked over the other machines, what have you found?"

Jimmy stuffed the Tasty Pie in his mouth and spoke

while he chewed. "It's like this," he said. "The deal is, twenty of these 'scopes came in about three months ago. I looked at every one of them, tested them out—two of them had bum switches. I sent them back. When they came back, we retested them—AOK—so when the 'scope upstairs went out, I asked Calvin to check out the insides, just to make sure."

"And did he?"

"Look, Doc. Calvin's a little spacy, but he doesn't bull-shit. He says he checked them out—he opened up every machine we got back."

"So how come the switch didn't work?"

"I don't know—sometimes they get stuck—sometimes you turn them in a hurry, you don't move them just the right way—these are sensitive machines."

Beauregard sighed deeply and tapped the wire on his desk. It was, the more he examined it, a pretty ragged clip mark.

"It's unbelievable," he said. "What you're telling me is that somebody clipped that thing after Calvin checked these machines—sometime right before the CCU death."

Jimmy wiped the strawberry filling from the Tasty Pie on his pants and picked at his teeth. Then he took a long swig of Yoo Hoo.

"Doc," he said matter-of-factly, "this thing is . . . I seen wires that were cut and I seen ones that were broke. This one was cut. That's all there is to it."

"Jesus!" Beauregard said, "This is too much. Jesus Christ!"

He sat down and stared at the wire.

"The only thing we don't know," Jimmy said, "is why anybody would cut it. Who would want to murder that old lady?"

"Jimmy," Beauregard said, "I've got to have time to think about this. So don't say a word to anyone."

Jimmy took a big hunk of pie and chewed with his mouth open.

"My mouth is full," he said, laughing and dropping some crust on Beauregard's floor.

17

The red light flashed on Beauregard's phone. He stared at it for a second, rubbed his hand over his cheeks, and sighed.

"Hello."

The voice was a falsetto, both comical and hysterical.

"Dr. Beauuuuregard. This is Charles."

"Charles who?"

"Charles—with Lauren Shaw. You know. I'm her personal assistant.

"Right, Charles. How are you?"

"I'm fine, Doctor. It's Lauren. She just collapsed."

Beauregard sucked in his breath. The minute he heard the words he knew he had secretly expected this call, and he cursed himself for not insisting she come into the hospital.

"When did this happen?"

"Just about a half hour ago," Charles said. "She was supposed to go onstage tonight, and we were running through some of the rewrites, and suddenly, with no warning whatsoever . . . Oh, God, it was so awful. I just started to scream. She just fell off the English library stairs that are in the second act."

"Charles, where is she now?"

"Well, in an ambulance, of course. You don't think we

124

just let her sluuuump there like a piece of furniture, do you?"

"She's coming into Emergency?"

"Well, of course."

"Good-bye, Charles."

Peter Cross opened the closet door to the armamentarium and pulled out his bag. Behind him two nurses walked by, their stiffly starched gowns rustling. "Have you heard? The actress Lauren Shaw has been admitted. They're making the diagnosis now. She's up in Room Two-twenty-eight."

Cross turned and watched them moving away from him. The fat one, dressed in white, looked like a nun or a penguin. He smiled at them, turned and started toward his OR, when he smashed into someone. When he regained his composure, he looked up and saw Harry Gardner.

"Hey, Spaceman," Harry said, "you got to keep the feet aligned with the brain. That's the way the animal works."

Cross looked down at the floor at his bag. It had fallen, and he heard a bottle break.

"It wasn't me who was running down the hall, Harry. Just watch it."

"Watch it? You getting a little testy, aren't you, Spaceman. Whatsamatter? That woman of yours keeping you up all night?"

Cross suddenly had the urge to smash Harry in the face with his bag. The asshole, the presumptuous, condescending ape. What made it worse was that he hadn't seen Debby in three days. But don't let the ape know he's getting to you.

"It beats banging June Boswell between shifts," Peter said, and then was immediately sorry he had let it slip.

Harry shot him a look like a bull on the rampage.

"What does that mean, Spaceman? You trying to say something?"

He reached over and grabbed Peter's lapel and pulled him toward him.

Peter smiled at him now, enjoying the game.

"No, Harry, should it?"

Gardner's breath was in his face. He smelled of relish, and Peter wanted to gag, but he looked him in the eye.

"I wouldn't go talking about June and me," Harry said. "I know what's been going around, and if you say anything . . ."

Peter took his hand and squeezed it. He could feel the fingers giving under his grip.

"Listen, Harry," he said, "if I were you, I'd keep a real low profile. Some of the more unscrupulous types around here are starting some real nasty rumors about you and June."

Harry's mouth dropped open in surprise.

Peter leered at him, and when he had removed Harry's hand from his lapel, he pushed him backward.

"Don't ever grab me again, Harry," he said. "You hear me? Don't come near me."

Harry rubbed his fingers and cracked his knuckles.

"Just kidding, Cross. I've been a little on edge."

"Yeah?" Peter said. "That's too bad."

He smiled again at Harry, and for the first time since Vietnam, Harry felt a shadow pass across his face. It was as if he had never seen Cross before, and now for the first time, the mask had been pulled off, revealing the grinning skull. He watched as Cross walked away. The long, powerful gliding stride. Something almost effeminate about it—but more than that, something he hadn't seen before—full of power, confidence.

He stood there, staring, transfixed, until Peter Cross

126

turned the corner. Then Harry rubbed his knuckles again and thought of what Dios had said before about Cross. There just might be something to it after all.

"Lauren. Lauren. Are you awake?"

Lauren Shaw looked up, and it was a moment before her eyes focused. She had just had her Demerol shot and was feeling groggy . . . pleasantly groggy, but the pleasantness was unsettling, for she realized that it masked something terrifying, something not pleasant at all. It was almost too much, the millions of betrayals the body could play on a person. And just when she was coming back, finding herself again . . . a smash play, film offers rolling in from the Coast. Now she blinked and stared at Robert Beauregard's handsome, reassuring face.

"Beau," she said hoarsely, reaching out and taking his hand.

He smiled and took her hand in his.

She smiled and looked just over his shoulder at a beautiful bouquet of roses which sat in a vase by the door.

"Beau, the flowers . . ."

"I brought them," he said. "The first, but not the last."

"That's sweet, Beau. I'm sorry to cause you so much trouble."

He smiled at her and sat down on the chair next to the bed.

"How does your head feel?" he asked.

"Much better. They gave me a shot of something."

"Demerol," Beauregard said, staring at her pupils. They seemed normal. Indeed, she looked radiant, as though she could get up and walk home.

"Beau, what is it?"

She looked at him dead on, wanting the truth.

"You've got an aneurysm, Lauren," he said. "Do you know what that is?"

She managed a smile.

"This is like a role I played once," she said. "The noble dying mother with the bloated blood vessel. They can pop any time, isn't that it?"

There was just the faintest touch of fear in her voice, and Beauregard admired the courage she was showing.

"One side of the vein simply gets tired. It's weakened, though we're not sure why it is. It puffs out, and it needs immediate attention."

"Where is it, Beau?"

"In the brain, Lauren. It's not an easy operation. But you're going to have the best person around. Dr. Spencer Taylor. He'll handle it all right. You're not to worry."

"Sure," said Lauren. "Come on, Beau. Forget the bedside manner. What are my chances?"

He smiled at her and held her hand again.

"Excellent," he said. "We've caught it in time. We're going to fix it up tomorrow."

"And if you don't get it?"

"We'll get it, Lauren. Three months from now you'll be out in Hollywood shooting a movie."

"Beau," she said. "With your charm, I should have you as my director."

She raised her eyebrow and winked at him.

"I've missed you, you know?"

Beauregard felt a pang of guilt. He should have called her. He should have done something. Christ—months had gone by—he knew about the pains... He sighed deeply, and for a second something flashed through his mind... another operating table... another brain operation. He saw the pleading face before him, his own hand on the oxygen tank.

"I've missed you too, Lauren," he said awkwardly.

She smiled and squeezed his hand.

"Poor Beau. Guilty until proven innocent. You judge

yourself too harshly. I'm glad that Heather is back. I know what she means to you. I'm happy for you, Beau. I really am. You're my dearest friend."

He smiled at her again and nodded slowly.

"And you mine," he said.

18

"Go ahead, jerk, dial the phone."

Debby sat in her apartment, staring at the tube. Richie Cunningham and Fonzie were playing a trick on Arnold. Debby picked up her drink—a large glass of vodka over ice—and suddenly wanted to hurl the whole thing at the screen. The goddamned 50's. Who would ever want to live through them? She remembered her brother Sam, his whinings about women . . . they tortured him so often that he ended up marrying a woman twice his age, just so he could finally get in the sack. They had lasted two years, been divorced, and now he spent all his money paying for her trips to St. Croix. But that was Sam all right. He was a product of his age. Not like you, Debby. Hey, you're in the swinging 70's where everybody is totally "up front" about sex. Hey, you're free of inhibitions, you can sleep with whomever you want. Pick up any magazine, turn on any TV show, and they are hitting you with the new morality . . . it's a swinger's paradise out there. Except the only man you want to swing with is Peter Cross.

And she hadn't seen him or heard from him since Saturday. Three days. Sunday wasn't too bad—she had spent it doing things around the apartment. Monday she was a little anxious. But things were going so well between them. Still no word. Once she called his apartment and let the phone ring and ring. No answer. He was not at the hospital; the desk said he'd called in sick. It had been so long since they hadn't spent their time off together that she was lost. The loneliness was opening up inside of her. Oh, God—what was going on with him?

On Tuesday—still no word. Oh, God, where is he? It was then that she pinpointed Peter's mood swing to the time spent in the wine cellar.

Enough of this shit, she thought. She walked into her bedroom—stared at the Miro print on the wall—so happy, carefree, a mockery of her melodramatic condition. She lay down, and in no time the tears were coming, though out in the living room she could hear the high-pitched cackle of the laugh track. Maybe that's what people needed with them. A recorded laugh track carried around with them. That way, when the guy you were in love with dumped you, you could just hit the playback button and hear it, "Hahahahaha," like a funhouse lady you heard in a cheap upstate carny, the one with the pig-squeal laugh that made you want to pound your temples and scream. What the hell had happened? Had she flirted with Beauregard? No, that was absurd. Even Peter hadn't delivered that pronouncement with any authority. No, he was upset by something else.

Back in the living room, she stared at Fonzie, who was going "Heyyyy," and she put her forefinger into her mouth, and bit off her nail. Christ, that was dumb. You've been growing that for a month. She looked down at the green telephone. If only he would call.

It came to her in a flash. It was totally against all tradition. It broke all the rules, but she was desperate. Peter would kill her if he knew she had been so bold as to call Dr. Beauregard. They all knew the way the system worked—the Indians did not take liberties with the chiefs. But, after all, it was Beau who had broken the ice, and certainly Heather had opened herself up to them.

"Hello."

"Heather, this is Debby."

"Well, Debby, how are you? I really enjoyed seeing you and Peter the other night."

"So did I, Heather . . . I really did. It was a terrific night . . . except . . ."

"Except for what?" Heather said.

Debby felt a pang of betrayal. She hadn't meant to get Heather involved at all. Now it was too late.

"Well," she said, "I really called to talk to Dr. Beauregard about it, but if you'll promise to keep it a secret, I guess I'd like to tell you both."

"Fire away," Heather said.

"It's about Peter. He was in such great spirits . . . up until he and Dr. Beauregard went into the wine cellar. Then, when he came back, his mood had changed."

"Yes," Heather said. "I'm really glad you called because I noticed it too. He seemed more reserved . . . a little tense."

"So you noticed it too," Debby said, picking up her drink. "Well, it got a lot worse. When we went home he was annoyed at me. I don't want to go into it. He just acted very tense. I just wondered if he and Beau . . . had some kind of disagreement in the cellar."

"Well," Heather said, "I'm afraid I can't tell you for sure. Beau hasn't mentioned anything about it to me, and he's out with Sarah right now. Taking her to dance class—and doing some shopping. But I'll ask him . . . though I rather doubt it. I'm sure he would have said something if anything unpleasant had occurred."

Debby felt foolish, embarrassed, inflicting her private life on such new friends.

132

"Heather, I'm sorry to bother you with this. It was silly of me."

"Not at all," Heather said. "If you want my opinion, I think your Mr. Cross is . . . well, perhaps I shouldn't say."

"No, do," Debby said.

"Well," Heather said, "I like Peter. I like him a lot. But he seems a little tense . . . and from what Beau has told me about him, I'd guess that he's been sort of a recluse most of his life. You know what I mean. He's like Beau in some ways . . . a total professional. He doesn't know how to relax properly. He doesn't trust himself in a social situation. And he has a certain contempt for it. So, the other night he was having a good time . . . then he suddenly realized he was having a good time. Maybe he felt he was having too good a time . . . so he got nervous, and a little defensive. I hope you don't mind my saying all this. It's a little out of line, I know, but I had a strong feeling about him as soon as we met. He seems to me the kind of man who needs to learn how to take it easy . . . to enjoy the lulls. I'd say that the other night was a start, but that he needs more time doing absolutely nothing."

Debby smiled and felt a tremendous kinship with Heather Beauregard. She was all Beau had said she was.

"You're right," Debby said. "That's it of course."

"I could be all wet," Heather said, "but I really think Peter is an extraordinary man, and like a lot of superior people, he just doesn't trust himself. It's as though his mind is years ahead of his other qualities. He's quite capable of being witty, intelligent, even eloquent—he just needs to trust people a little more—and most of all to relax."

"Yes," Debby said, "that's true. But why hasn't he called me?"

"Oh, come on," Heather said. "You know men. He

probably feels like a fool for throwing a tantrum in front of you, and he's too embarrassed to make up. You ought to call him, and . . . I don't know exactly . . . maybe go away together, by yourselves, and just enjoy one another. That would probably be just the thing."

"It would," Debby said. "I know it would. And I know just the spot."

Heather laughed heartily. "Glad to help," she said. "I think you've got to understand, with men like Beau and Peter, you're always in a very real war with the hospital. It gets to be an obsession with them. It can even become a kind of psychosis. But a little R and R will do you both a world of good. So get the guy and take him to your lair."

Debby laughed again.

"Thanks, Heather," she said. "Thanks, really . . ."

"Advice is easy," Heather said. "Getting that dynamo to calm down might be a little work. But I've got faith in you. I can tell you one thing, he likes you very, very much."

"The feeling is mutual," Debby said. "Well, thanks again."

"My honor," Heather said. "Bye."

"Bye."

Debby sat on the couch and looked across the green rug at the TV. She smiled to herself and dialed Peter Cross. This time when he didn't answer she was calm. She'd just keep on calling until he showed up.

134

19

Harry Gardner felt the air in the room congealing on him. He had to keep cool, calm down ... get his drugs ready. Across from him two Filipino nurses laughed cheerfully and Gardner envied them. He wished to hell it was one of them instead of himself going in here. But that was no way to feel. He should be happy that he drew Lauren Shaw's case. She was certainly one of the most famous persons the hospital had ever had. Ordinarily, he would see it as a great chance to make an impression on the staff. Hell, if he played his cards right, he might even get to know her after the operation. But still his hand shook a little as he lined up the drugs in his armamentarium—the Innovar, sodium pentothal, the Fentanyl, and the Arfonad, which would lower her blood pressure. Still, there was nothing particularly terrifying about the operation. She would come through it okay. An aneurysm wasn't any joke, but Dr. Taylor was the best around. There shouldn't be any real problem. Relax, he told himself, and stop thinking of June, or of Beauregard. Still, it was tough, for he knew that Beauregard would be watching him from the TV room on the second floor. Keeping a close watch. He knew damned well that Beauregard would have preferred to have Cross on the case, but Cross had been out with the flu for two days, so he had drawn the assignment. So relax. He picked up his bag, snapped it shut, and left the Prep Room to go to the OR.

"Hey, Harry," Spencer Taylor said as Harry came through the door, "you're a star."

"Yeah," Harry said. He went over and checked the pop-off valve in the anesthesia machine, then quickly went over the other equipment. Everything was in order. He laid a tray down and set out his drugs on it. Then behind him Lauren Shaw was wheeled into the room. She was already nearly under.

"Hello, Dr. Gardner," she said, dazed.

"Hello, Miss Shaw. You feel all right?"

"Never better. You know they gave me some very nice drugs to help me sleep."

"Relax, Miss Shaw. We're going to have you back on the stage in no time."

Dr. Taylor smiled at her and held her hand.

"It's going to be fine," he said.

"Okay," Harry said. "Let's get her up on the table."

The two scrub nurses helped Lauren Shaw off the portable and onto the table.

"Time to relax," Harry said.

He opened the airways for her and then turned on the anesthesia machine. Meanwhile, he got the Innovar ready—1 cc. of it, and quickly injected it into the IV. In a matter of seconds, Lauren Shaw was under, and they began to place her face in the Mayfield head rest, which allowed her head to be held tightly by two pins in the occipital area, and another in the frontal area. They tilted her head slightly to the right, the left side facing up, and then the nurse began to shave her. Harry looked down and let out a long sigh.

"Jesus, I hate to see that," Beauregard said.

He sat in the darkened room along with the other doc-

136

tors watching the TV monitor. In front of him a cigarette burned, and he realized how nervous he was. He wished Cross were handling this. Then he realized that Cross had been out for a couple of days. He should have called him, but the boy had been strangely cold during the dinner. He had meant to say something to Peter about it, but things had happened too fast. Dr. Dios sat on the other side of him, drinking some apple juice.

"Harry will do a good job," Dios said to one of the others. "And Taylor . . . She's going to be fine."

Beauregard's sentiments exactly. So why was he sweating so much?

"We'll leave her some hair," Dr. Taylor said. "As much as we can. Then she can get a wig for a while."

The nurse, Peggy Schmidt, smiled.

"We cannot let the *Post* get hold of this. It would ruin her career."

Harry watched as they finished prepping her head, then he injected some Innovar.

"Just a kiss," he said. "Make her relaxed."

He watched as she relaxed, checked her blood pressure. Everything was normal. Then Taylor and his assistant, Moss, slid their headlights over their eyes. Harry stared at them. He never quite got used to those big spotlights. It always seemed as if they were a couple of miners going after the mother lode.

"Towels, please."

The nurses and Taylor draped the patient's head with green towels, and then the nurse stitched the towels to her scalp. And Harry injected a touch of xylocaine locally, just to stop the bleeding. Then the doctors and the nurses hooked up the suction devices and the electric coagulation instruments.

Finally, Taylor looked over at Harry.

"Is everything ready?"

"Steady," Harry said.

"Okay, then we're going in."

Beauregard sighed again. Harry had done a very competent job. In fact, better than competent. Perhaps he had been too tough on Harry, just as they all seemed to be too tough on Peter. The important thing was the quality of a man's work. It was going to be fine. Behind him the door opened, and when Beauregard turned, he saw Cross come into the room. He motioned to him, and Peter made his way through the chairs and found a seat.

"Peter, how are you?" Beauregard said.

"Okay now. I had a couple of shots . . . got some rest. I'm going to work tonight for a few hours. Get crazy hanging around the apartment. I wish I could have been in on this one."

"Frankly, so do I. But Harry seems to be doing a fine job."

"He's a good man," Peter said. "A very good man."

Dr. Taylor started the horseshoe-shaped incision on Lauren Shaw's scalp. A neat, curving arc, which cut away the flesh. Then behind him Moss brought up the drill, and they started in working on the four burr holes. The first one was just above the zygomatic process. Harry watched as the tissue opened, the blood spilling a little. The sound of the drill always got to him. He watched as they started the second one in the frontal area, and then the third in the parietal bone, and finally number four in the temporal bone, a few inches above the ear. Harry heard the bone being chipped away and thought of termites . . . the Roto-Rooter Boys, they sometimes called it, though not today, for everyone was well aware that Beauregard was watching every move and listening to every comment. There was going to be no black humor today, for certain. Harry checked the blood pressure, his drip, the heart machine. Quickly they were inside her skull, looping the holes together from hole to hole. Then they lifted the scalp off and the dura was exposed.

"Okay," Taylor said, "which way do you think we should go in?"

"I would think this way," Moss said, indicating a semicircular direction. "That way the brain will be right in front of us."

"Okay," Taylor said. "That makes sense."

They began to work their way in, and Harry watched as the skull was lifted completely away. In front of him was Lauren Shaw's brain—the Sylvian fissure, that dividing line between the frontal and the temporal lobes.

"Well," Taylor said, "we know it's in the depth of the Sylvian fissure at the origin of the middle cerebral artery."

"We've got to go very slowly here. Bring me the microscope."

"Here they go," Beauregard said. He was aware of Peter's breath next to him.

"You all right?" he said.

"Yes," Peter said. "I'm fine. Just fine."

He stuck his hand in his pocket, fidgeted around, and stared at the TV as though he were watching a priest in some ancient ritual. Beauregard bit his lip and watched and smoked.

Harry watched as Taylor draped the microscope and looked down into Lauren Shaw's brain. Taylor took the knife and slowly, millimeter by millimeter, began to dissect the Sylvian fissure. He could feel the tension in the room, and yet, he could tell the way things were going that it wasn't as tough as they had thought.

"It's okay," Taylor said. "I've reached the aneurysm. It's not that bad. We can clip it. But I need that hypotensive drug now, Harry. I want her blood pressure as low as possible."

Harry smiled at the nurse. He was going to come out of this smelling like a rose.

He reached for the Arfonad bottle and hung it up on the IV pole. He then took a 20-gauge needle and introduced it into the main IV line, after which he slowly opened the stopcock of the Arfonad bottle and let it begin to drip in. He looked up and saw it working, then checked the blood pressure. Everything was okay.

"It's all right," Harry said. "Pressure should drop in a second."

He turned and looked at the pressure gauge. Impossible . . . it was impossible. Her pressure was actually rising.

"Hey," he said, "I don't get it. Her pressure is going up."

"What the hell did you put in there?" Taylor said.

"Arfonad," Harry said. He looked at the label on the bottle. "It's weird."

Her blood pressure was rising . . . rising . . .

"Get that out of there," Taylor said.

Harry stood stunned. He stared at the blood pressure. "It's up to two-ten," he said meekly. "Christ."

Taylor pushed him out of the way and pulled the bottle off the line.

"Jesus," he said. "Jesus! She can't take this. Get a new bottle of Arfonad quick. I don't think she can take it. The vessel is getting huge. Oh, shit!"

There was suddenly a tremendous popping noise, almost like a balloon, and a bright clot of blood showered Dr. Taylor and Harry Gardner.

140

"Jesus!"

The two men watched helplessly as Lauren Shaw's brain began to bulge out of the open skull, like toothpaste oozing out of a tube.

"Fentanyl," Harry shouted, trying desperately to inject it in the IV.

But it was too late. The aneurysm had burst, and the brain splattered all over the floor. One of the nurses screamed, and the other grabbed her and held her. Harry stood back, staring at Lauren Shaw's bald and broken head. He felt as though he were in a movie. That someone would yell, "Cut"; say, "Great job." It was all just a play ... it had to be. But then Dr. Taylor and Moss were grabbing him, and suddenly, he saw Beauregard racing into the room, and there were the horrified shouts of people in the hall, and he was being led, forcibly, his arms pinned behind him, out of the operating room.

20

Cross watched them take Harry Gardner out on the TV. All the others had raced down to the OR to see what was happening, but there was no hurry now . . . no hurry at all. He felt a relaxation, a wonderful fluid sensation all over himself. The Space was pleased, very pleased. He smiled and waited until the commotion had died down. Then he left the TV room and went down the hall, taking the back steps down to his office. Quickly he went inside and shut the door. He sat down on the old cane chair he had brought with him from Baltimore.

He reached into his right pocket and found the four empty ampules of norepinephrine. God, it had worked beautifully, so beautifully. It pumped the vein up just like pure adrenaline. He thought of her brain splattering, the way it had looked . . . like a painting against the wall. Then suddenly he was seized by panic. The four bottles in his lab pocket . . . hadn't they originally been five. He reached into his other pocket, but it was empty. No, maybe there hadn't been five. He had to remember . . . Recall.

He thought of the morning. Coming in early . . . waiting for Harry to go into the Prep Room and fill up his drip bottle with Arfonad and dextrose and water. Then he had gone out to the pay phone and called into the hospital paging system. An important call for Dr. Harry Gardner. He then went back and had waited, hidden in the washing room, and as soon as Harry had come out, he had taken the bottles—four of them—yes, it was four . . . taken them out, and put them into his own bottle. He had then carried that bottle into the Prep Room and carefully peeled off the tape from Harry's bottle and placed it on his own. Harry's bottle he had brought back here to the office.

Now he looked at the bottle which sat on his desk under a towel. Careless of him to leave it there. If someone had come in—but they hadn't—because he was immune now. June would crack . . . admit that she was with Harry . . . and they would link him up with the other murder . . . say that he killed Esther Goldstein as well. He was in the clear . . . free to do his work . . . and Harry would swing for it. He loved it, he loved it all. All his life, ever since the playgrounds of Baltimore, the jocks, the Harrys of the world had shit on him, and now it was his turn. He had just started to work. They had no idea of what he was capable of. For that matter, he was not sure himself, but it would be bold. He was through feeling sorry for himself, through with sentimentality. He had done it. He felt like screaming it out down the white halls . . .

Instead, he grabbed the four empty norepinephrine bottles, and Harry's drip bottle of Arfonad, stuck them in his armamentarium, snapped the case shut, and left the office. In two minutes he was downstairs in the parking lot. And in another five he was sailing down the East Side Drive, looking with pleasure on the bright, bountiful sky.

"You have the right to remain silent and to refuse to answer questions. Anything you say may be used in a court of law against you. You have the right to consult an attorney before speaking to the police, or to have an attorney present now or in the future. If you do not have an attorney . . ."

Harry Gardner looked up at the prancing figure hovering above him in the small dust-filled room. He couldn't quite square the voice and the character of Detective Frank Lombardi with the situation.

The room was station house chic—scarred, peeling walls, a beaten-up old desk, a picture of a bearded man with intense olive-colored eyes and flaring nostrils. But Lombardi himself looked more like Beau Brummel than a detective. His threads were obviously first class—a light green suit, green-and-white checked body shirt, and a solid green wool tie. On his feet, the feet which flashed up and down the dusty room, were black Italian boots.

"You have heard your rights," Lombardi said. "Now, are you willing to cooperate?"

Harry turned to Beauregard, who was staring at him as though he were a bug.

"I told you from the beginning I was willing to cooperate," he said. "So what's the problem? I didn't do it. It's that simple."

"Oh?" Lombardi said. He took out a monogrammed handkerchief and blew his nose. His eyes watered a little.

Beau couldn't keep quiet. "Look, Gardner, Lauren Shaw's brain burst from an overdose of norepinephrine. Norepinephrine, Harry. A drug that causes the blood pressure to rise—in an aneurysm case. Jesus!" He couldn't go on. He was numb from it all, numb from the sight of Lauren's beautiful mind spilled over the OR walls, numb from the fact that one of his anesthesiologists had pumped a drug into her veins that killed her—right before his eyes.

"Somebody switched bottles on me," Harry said. "It

144

had to be that."

"Nah," Lombardi said. He took out some Visine and squeezed a couple of drops into his eyes.

"Sinuses," he said. "Tough. I was just getting ready to go over to Italy for my annual shopping tour. Get myself some new Bugatti outfits . . . maybe a couple Georgio Armani sportswear things . . . and this comes up. Ah, killers have such a bad sense of timing."

Harry clenched his teeth, and Beauregard let out a long breath and ran his hand through his graying hair.

"I'm telling the truth. There was a switch."

"A switch, huh?" Lombardi said. "You're talking pure moviesville."

He turned and looked at Beauregard.

"An interesting phenomenon. I was thinking about maybe doing a book on the subject. All these guys, criminal types, use plots they copped from TV. Then they come in and use TV alibis, and half the time it works. Only not in this precinct. We all spend a great deal of time keeping up with crime. Watch old Kojaks every week. So maybe you better run through this all again, huh, pal?"

Harry opened his hands and dropped his head.

"I'm telling you," he said.

There was a knock at the door, and Beefy Sloan, a big cop with a face that would put out the sun, came in. Behind him were two of the hospital's administrators, Gamble and Blake. They were both red-faced men in their fifties, and they wore identical pinstripes.

"Nice suits," Lombardi said to them. "Brown's of London?"

"Saville Row," Gamble said.

"The older generation," Lombardi said.

Gamble raised one eyebrow and Blake rolled his eyes. Then they both stared hard at Harry Gardner.

"You just made it in time," Lombardi said. "He's about to crack."

Beauregard started to protest. He didn't much like Lombardi and he was having trouble keeping the image of Lauren's last moments out of his mind. He wanted very much to at least understand what had happened, to be able to deal with it, but Lombardi's methods of interrogation made the whole affair seem like a shot on the "Tonight Show."

"Now about this call?" Lombardi said. "You say you got a call right before you went into the room?"

"That's right," Harry said. "I got a call. He could have switched the drugs then."

"Yeah," Lombardi said. "He could have. Or you could have had a friend at a bar call you ... maybe Dios."

"Dios?" said Harry. "Dios? Ask him if you think that. Look, I came down here without a lawyer because I'm innocent. I'm telling you I had a call and it wasn't from Dios."

"No," Lombardi said, opening his tie and using the Visine again. "It's so sunny in Italy right now ... so warm ... But you are quite right. It wasn't Dios. We already talked with him, you see ... and all he told us was about how you and he had talked about Vietnam."

"What?" Harry said.

He looked at Lombardi in complete amazement. Gamble and Blake shifted uneasily in their seats. Lombardi looked at the big detective.

"Go get me some Rolaids," he said. "This is making me sick."

"Vietnam," Harry said.

"Yeah, he said you used to talk about 'greasing' people in Vietnam. He said he was outraged by the idea, but you said you didn't mind it at all."

"But it wasn't like that," Harry said. "I mean, I never

146

said anything like that. I was saying in combat conditions... Besides... you ask him... you ask Dios about Peter Cross. Dios was always suspicious of Cross. Dios will tell you."

"Tell us what? I've got a signed statement from him, Dr. Gardner. It says that you and he talked about greasing people. It doesn't mention anything about any Peter Cross."

"That bastard," Harry said. "He thought Cross killed the old lady... and then the second one... that Mrs. Goldstein... he talked to me again about it."

"Yeah," Lombardi said, rubbing a Kleenex across his boots. He stopped and looked at Beauregard. "You like these? Joceyln of Paris. You think all cops are going to look like Columbo? I teach at NYU, I got book deals."

Beauregard looked over at the two administrators. Gamble was smiling widely. Blake's eyes looked as blank as Raisinets.

"Let's see," Lombardi said. "You were saying something about being seen in the building? Well, I've had about twenty very tired men hanging out at the hospital all day, and we came up with a couple of very interesting documents."

Lombardi stopped, blew his nose, and cleared his throat. He reached into his desk and pulled out a folder, opened it, and came around to the front of the desk. Gardner looked at him, a neat, compact body like a dancer's. He was an entertainer, but he was tough, there was no mistaking that. Cut through you like a nail file.

"Now, according to these extremely interesting documents," Dr. Gardner, "you were seen with one June Boswell on the night of Esther Goldstein's death."

"No."

"No?" Lombardi looked at the three men with open-mouthed surprise. "Are you saying no?"

“I wasn’t there,” Harry said.

“You weren’t there?”

“I mean . . .”

“Yes?”

Harry glanced over at Beauregard, who sat tensely in his chair. The dust flew through the room, and the sunlight faded.

“Maybe you’re going to tell us to ask June,” Lombardi said. “Well, don’t bother. We already asked her, and she got all upset. She used about four of my monogrammed handkerchiefs—made expressly for me by an old peasant lady in Barcelona—I might bill her . . .”

He smiled like a happy, sensual sadist.

“On the other hand, her performance was so good, I might not. She had a lot to say. Why, it was so interesting we not only wrote it down, we taped it. Maybe we’ll play it on the radio . . . True Confessions.”

He motioned to the big cop with the broken nose and the dumb lips.

“Go get the Academy Award,” he said.

There was utter silence. Harry Gardner felt something happening to his windpipe. He couldn’t breathe at all, and yet he was afraid to gasp for air. It might make him look guilty. He shut his eyes and saw Peter Cross’s face staring at him. The little smile on his face the day they had had their scene in the hall. Cross. Dios had been right, but now Dios was copping out, selling him down the river. He should never have trusted him. Christ . . . and now June . . .

The big cop brought in the tape and handed it to Lombardi.

“Thanks, Beefy,” he said. “Now . . . let’s see if we can all tune in on this.”

He switched the Play button and in a moment there was a loud wailing which shot through the room. Everyone jumped and Harry felt as if he were falling through the floor.

"Sorry," Lombardi said, adjusting the volume button. "Now, let's see here."

"I don't want to talk about Harry," June said. "He's always been a friend of mine."

"Yes," said Lombardi's voice, "a dear true friend. We understand that. Only there is a problem here. He might have killed people. So why don't you tell us about the night you got sick."

"I already told everybody," June said. Her voice cloudy, thick . . . drunk or on pills.

"Just once more, dear," Lombardi said. "We have to hear it just once more. How you went to the ladies' room, only it wasn't the ladies' room, because you were coming down the wrong hallway. Now, how did that happen?"

Harry Gardner bit his lower lip as June began to sob.

"What do you want me to say?" she said, sounding like a little girl.

"Just the truth," Lombardi said, sounding like the elementary school principal.

"God . . . he's always been so sick . . . so sick . . . I don't know . . . I just don't know . . . I don't want to lose my job . . . I've always been a good nurse . . . and it's . . ."

The four men sat rigid, embarrassed by her sobs.

"It's because I want to do right that I'm going to tell you . . . even though it's my job . . . I had it for Harry . . . I knew he wasn't any good, but I couldn't help it . . . He was fun, exciting . . . all right, I'll tell you . . . he turned me on . . . He wasn't a wimp . . . I don't know . . . Maybe I'm sick . . . But he turned me on . . . I hadn't been able to get turned on for a long time . . . Men in New York . . . I don't know . . . He would come up every once in a while . . . right after the patients were asleep . . . you

know, right after I'd just checked them . . . and we'd go
. . . oh, shit, I don't believe I'm telling you this . . . I
can't believe I'm saying this . . . I used to be such a nice
girl . . . I used to wear a blue and white dress to Catholic
high school."

Beauregard felt such a loathing for Harry that he
wanted to reach across the room and throttle him. He
made his hand into a tight fist.

"All right . . . I might as well tell you . . . He'd come up
and we'd go into the room . . . the old room where they
have the equipment . . . you know the old stuff . . . some
of the gases . . . the cyclopropane . . . Harry used to make
a joke about that stuff . . . said if we really made it good
. . . whammm . . . the whole place . . . anyway, he came
with me the night she died . . . We went back there, and
Harry musta been tired or drunk or something. He
couldn't get off . . . He tried, then he got nasty . . . I mean
we used to just play at bondage and stuff . . . Oh, Jesus,
I know how it sounds now . . . but it was just playing
around . . . you know . . . pretending . . . It was like a turn-
on . . . I never thought for a second he was really into it
. . . Or maybe I did . . . But only a little . . . for an extra
kick . . . Jesus, I know how this must sound . . ."

Lombardi clicked the machine off. Beauregard stared
at Harry with immense hatred. Harry sighed and
squirmed in his chair.

Now Lombardi reached into his desk and pulled out
the piece of red wire Beauregard had given to him. He
showed it to Harry. Harry blinked uncomprehendingly.

"Surprised?" Lombardi said. "You're surprised to see
this?"

"What?" Harry said. He reached for it and looked it
over. "What the hell is this?"

"That? You don't know? Oh, this is good. Real
Richard Diamond stuff. That is the beeper signal from

the oscilloscope you cut . . . so that there was no warning.
You killed that old lady. Then, before June could read
the EKGs, you hustled her off for some sex. Like to get it
on after, hey?"

"No," Harry said. "I've never seen this before. Never."

"Heard you were pretty good as a greaser in 'Nam."

Harry suddenly got a glimpse of the person behind the
wise-ass jokes and outlandish clothes. Either this guy
was pushing him to the limit as a ploy or he was convinced that Harry was guilty—and if he was guilty it
meant he had to have something, something more than a
tape and a wire.

"But the first one," Harry said, "Peter Cross killed
her. He was in the OR."

"Sure," Lombardi said. "You switched drugs on him.
Then later, when the doctors went over it, they quoted
you as saying how weird Cross is. You want to make a
statement now?"

"You think I switched drugs on Cross? That's crazy
. . . crazy. I'm telling you if there's anybody that could do
it, it's Cross. He has it in for me."

"Why's that?" Beauregard suddenly snapped.

Harry looked up at the eyes boring into him. He suddenly felt very scared. Clearly, they were railroading him,
only too glad to cover the whole thing up before it got any
further. He wanted to tell them that he had made fun of
Cross's girl, but he suddenly became cold in the arms. If
he said that, Beauregard would get pissed—fucking
Beauregard always protected Cross. No, there had to be
another way. If it was Cross, then he had to bring them
proof.

"I don't want to talk any more about it," Harry said.
"Not without a lawyer. And if you want me here, then
you'd better book me."

Lombardi slapped his hands together in glee and

moved swiftly around the desk.

"You'd better book me. Beautiful. Right out of Kojak. See what a service TV does. Gives the criminal class a little penny-ante training in law."

He turned to Gardner.

"We can't book you just yet, Gardner. We've got to hear from the Medical Examiner. But I don't think that will be long. You can leave for now, but I wouldn't try to run anywhere."

"Don't worry about it," Harry said, staring at the floor.

Gamble and Blake got up and began to smooth out their suits with their chubby hands.

"See you, Harry," Lombardi said.

He walked out into the outer office, Gamble, Blake, and Beauregard trailing him.

"That's all for now," Lombardi said to the two administrators. "But I think we just might have him."

"Thank you, Lieutenant," Gamble said, licking his lower lip. "It's always good to meet a professional."

"And a man of fashion," said Blake.

When he smiled, his mouth looked like ripped fabric.

The two men walked out, and Beauregard looked back in at Harry, who sat motionless, still staring at his feet.

"I hope we got him," Beauregard said. "I hope we nail him."

Lombardi smiled at him, patted him on the arm, and nodded his head.

"He isn't so tough," Lombardi said.

Beauregard smiled and turned to leave. But he could feel, even fifteen feet away, the penetrating green eyes of the lieutenant trained on a circle on his back.

21

Harry Gardner sat on an oak stool in the window of the Café Lafitte. He nursed a warm beer and stared out intently at the second-floor light which burned in the window on the opposite corner. Peter Cross's window. The light had been burning for two days nonstop, and Cross had not come out. Harry had called the hospital and found out from June (who became hysterical when she heard his voice) that Cross had called in sick. That was all he needed to hear. They nail him, and one day later, Peter Cross has a quick relapse of the flu. It smelled bad, and he was grateful for it, for anything that might get him somewhere.

He looked at the black tape recorder he had brought with him—a little Craig model—maybe tapes weren't admissible, but he'd get something out of Cross. He would if it killed him. But the thing was, he wasn't certain how to proceed. Cross wasn't any pushover... he was sure of that now. He had to take his time. But time was running out. Any day now the Medical Examiner would give his report, and they'd be indicting him. He had to make Cross screw up. The only sign so far was the light. He had seen Cross from the telephone booth across the street, the night before. Cross walking to and fro in front of the pale green curtains. The guy had insomnia. Of course, from a guilty conscience. It was clear. But he had to have more than that to go on. He thought about breaking into his apartment, searching for a clue. Maybe he was like the kooks you read about who kept a scrapbook of their victims—or made notes. He remembered his pinpoint eyes the other day, glaring at him.

It's better than banging June Boswell between shifts. A strange way to phrase it. Yes, it might have looked like it was between shifts to someone who had been hanging out for a while, didn't know if Harry was on or off.

Harry exhaled the cigarette smoke and watched the window.

Then he felt somebody rubbing his arm.

"What'sa matter, sweetie?"

Harry looked down at the aging bohemian woman and felt sick. She wore a black sweater, a dark black shirt, and her hair was tied back in the mandatory shopping-bag-lady ponytail. Her face was streaked badly with rouge, and her lipstick was on her gums. Her breath smelled like old dead vegetables, and Harry felt a strong urge to gag.

"Hey, there?" she said, "you a poet?"

"No," Harry said, "I'm not."

"Come on, stud," she said, "I've seen you in here before. You're that body-building poet. I know it, honey. You can't lie to Ruth Ann."

She hooked her old arm through his and breathed in his face.

"Look, ma," he said, "I'm busy, so buzz off."

"Ma?" she said, cackling like a goat. "Ma? Who the hell you talking to? I know e.e.—I know Bill de Kooning . . . you hear me. Who the hell?"

He pushed her away, and she fell back heavily on the floor. An elderly-looking man with gray hair and a red

154

bandana raced over and picked her up.

"You asshole," he said to Harry. "We don't need your kind of crap here. Hold on to me, Ruth Ann."

Harry opened his hands, trying to be conciliatory. The cops were the last thing he needed now. Quickly he looked back out the window and saw someone coming out of Cross's building, carrying a black bag. He looked again, pressing his nose up against the glass. The guy was moving fast. Looking to his right and left. Christ, it was Cross, and he was heading for the subway stop... no, a cab. He was getting a cab.

"Excuse me," Harry said, starting for the door, but the old lady was up now, grabbing onto him.

"Forget what Walter said, honey," she said. "I like your style."

He pushed her again, this time into the old man, and both of them tumbled backward into the bar, over a stool, and fell in a heap.

As he got outside, Harry saw Cross getting into a yellow cab and he began to run down the street after it. The bag... It might have evidence. Then it hit him. Cross had a car... Why wouldn't he take it? Unless he didn't want to be recognized. Harry raced down the block to Hudson Street, waved at a Checker. The cabbie ground gears and pulled to a stop. Quickly, Harry leaped inside.

"Ten bucks if you follow that cab," Harry said.

The man turned and looked at Harry, and smiled. "Allen Funt, right?"

"Come on," Harry said, flashing the ten, "I'm serious."

Harry leaned up against the wire cage, peered out through it and the glass. This was what it was going to be like, he thought, as Cross's cab wove ahead of them, going uptown. If he didn't catch Cross now, he was going to be looking through this steel grating for the rest of his life.

"Where the hell is he?" Harry said, rattling the cage.

"Relax, pal," the driver said, "just take your time and relax. It's going to be fine. You see over there . . . behind that parked truck."

Harry looked at the street—Times Square with its piles of human garbage. An old woman in a flowered print dress sat in front of him, with her fingers stuck in a black hole that nearly resembled a mouth. Up above her a black whore rattled her necklace and let her pocketbook hit the woman on the head, but the woman seemed not to notice. Everywhere the sounds of screaming sirens, pinballs, blaring music . . . and just on the other side of the street, a theater with the purple sign <LIVE SEX ACTS—MARGARITA and ROBERTO with his BIG 12-INCH> Just in front he saw the truck, and beyond it, next to the curb, the tail end of the Checker.

Then he had to duck down a little because Cross was getting out and heading inside.

"All right," the driver said, "we got him."

"Yeah," Harry said, barely aware of the driver, barely aware of the midget blowing his nose on the street, of the three Puerto Rican boys with tan slacks, identical powder-blue sports shirts, and golf clubs. He was focused on Cross, who was going up to the window. Yes, Cross, still holding the bag. Harry handed the driver his ten dollars and got out of the cab.

"Good luck," the cabbie said. "I hope you get him, pal."

Harry was moving now through the streets, dodging in and out of traffic. A double-decker English bus pulled in front of him as he made it to the island near the theater ticket booth. He dodged in between the crowd and saw

156

Cross enter the theater; then there was a lull in the traffic, and he was by a man who was holding out watches. "New watch, Bro. Check it out!" He made it up to the window and took his ticket from a boy-girl with orange punk hair and rouge.

Harry walked up the ramp, stepped in some caramel candy, and felt it cling to his shoes, pulling him back. He shook it off, then entered the theater. The house lights were off. Only a spotlight shone on the couple on stage. Harry stumbled ahead. Shit! He had to move carefully.

He stood still for a second, letting his eyes accustom themselves to the darkness. In front of him in an acne-red light, the boy stood over the woman, who knelt in front of him, taking his penis into her mouth. Harry blinked and looked around. Slowly, the shapes in front of him became distinguishable. There was an older man in the back row, eating a giant salami. He grunted as he cut off the slices with an old kitchen knife and held them over his mouth as though each one were a bunch of grapes. Then he let them slide in. They looked to Harry like silver dollars. The man was swallowing money.

He looked to his right. Two people in the row—one of them a woman, the other a tall man—could Cross be meeting someone here? He went down the row behind them and sat down in the chair. No, the man wasn't Cross, but a thin man with a crew cut and wire glasses. Suddenly music began to play the Bee Gee's hit "Stayin' Alive," and Harry saw the girl was swinging back and forth from the end of the man's cock, in time to the music.

He moved up another row, slowly, methodically . . . checking out each person. A fat man in a business suit was sitting with the *Post* over his lap. The newspaper was rising, and the man was making noises as though he were hyperventilating. Harry crawled down the row, moved on. Then he saw Cross clearly . . . sitting under the red exit sign . . . the bag sitting next to him. Harry moved forward, slowly, one row at a time. He wanted to come up on Cross from behind. Yes, the maximum surprise. The lights changed, and Harry blinked, saw the boy getting out a long whip, heard the girl's cries, "No, no." Then he looked over at Cross. He was up, out of his seat, holding the bag, and moving toward the exit. Harry got up, stumbled over a bottle of MD 2020 wine, and quickly followed him. The creep was heading out into the alley. Sure, he was going to ditch the stuff and then come back in for the show. Oh, clever, very clever. For three nights he had watched Cross, and now, now it had finally paid off. He felt himself gathering together, his muscles bunching tightly, the way he used to feel before a kickoff. It was going to be good to get the Space Cadet.

He reached the cold steel exit door and pulled it back, then walked out into the blue-light dark. He stared at the end of the alley and saw that it went around a corner. There were some trash cans in front of him, but around the corner he could hear a clanging sound. He moved forward down the alley, his fists swinging by his sides, his teeth clenched, his legs moving in short, violent strides. Yes, he had him.

Then suddenly Harry Gardner felt something around his throat, something strong, and before he could turn, something else bashed at his skull. He heard the sound like a pineapple being whacked and he tried to turn, but the blue light was going out fast. In one last burst of adrenaline, he managed to make the turn and claw at Cross, who stood in front of him now, holding a lead pipe.

Harry tried to grab at it but missed; it seemed to be

158

everywhere at once, smashing him, and he fell down to his knees, saying, "Cross, you bastard . . . Cross . . ." But when he looked up again, there was a syringe coming down toward his neck, and he screamed as Cross pulled him by the hair and injected the needle into the carotid artery.

Cross stood above him, smiling now, nodding and saying, "You wouldn't leave me alone would you? You'd hound me, wouldn't you? And then you'd try the hard stuff. Isn't that right Harry? Guys like you always get around to the hard stuff, twisting arms and breaking faces."

Peter thought of the phone call, of Harry waiting and watching for two days outside his apartment. He knew Harry would put the pieces together eventually, but there'd be no Harry to put them together for the cops.

Harry tried to grab the needle, but the potassium had hit him full force, and he fell over on his back like an injured insect, his arms and legs jerking in spasms.

"You thought you were following me here, didn't you Harry? What a stupid bastard you are. You thought it was Spaceman Cross on the run."

Cross knelt down beside the now inert Gardner, injecting the rest of the potassium into his neck, and then Peter felt his hands relaxing, his whole body flooded with warmth. His heart felt filled up, free of the hollow space, and he felt his face flush, his loins jerking, and he was a little embarrassed like that, to appear that way in front of Harry, but it felt good to feel so in control of things. Then he picked up Harry's body, carried it to the end of the alley where his own car was parked. He had left it there this morning. Of course, it was risky. Harry seemed the perfect patsy, but he knew the Harry's of the world. They would just keep coming, unless you stopped them. Besides, he had to do it. It was a score he had to settle with all the Harrys who had humiliated him his entire life. He was seized then with a momentary flash of panic. Maybe he had let himself get out of hand. Christ, they would have convicted Harry . . . but no. No, it would be just as he had said. He would get rid of him. They'd assume he was guilty and had jumped bail, fled. It was going to be all right.

Quickly, he opened the car door and began dragging Harry inside. He was heavy, terribly heavy, but Cross felt his own arms were suddenly those of a man twice his size. God, he was strong, stronger than this ape. No matter what happened it was worth it. He wished his father could see him now. In a few minutes he had Harry Gardner propped up. He spent a few seconds looking into the large, terrified eyes. There was such pain there, such hatred and stupidity. To think Gardner thought he could outwit Peter. The ape . . . the presumptuous ape.

Cross went around to the driver's side, and checked out his face in the rear view. A nasty scrape down the cheek. The one thing he hadn't counted on. He pulled out a Kleenex, and dabbed at it. Not too bad really. It could pass as a shaving cut. He started the engine of the car, and suddenly Harry slumped over on him, making Cross gasp. Gently, he moved Harry back to the passenger's seat. Time for a trip old friend, down the West Side Highway. The Apeman and the Space Cadet go for a midnight spin. Like an old serial on a faded Baltimore screen. The final frame of which would see Harry slowly, beautifully, falling off the rotting pier into the dark waiting waters below.

22

She sat at the bar, slumping over like a manikin, sipping her fourth vodka and tonic. Behind her on the jukebox she could hear the Bee Gee's chirping away about staying alive, and she began to giggle a bit. She was acting like a goddamned adolescent, not at all the liberated woman she had intended to become when she moved to New York.

She looked down the bar and saw a man with the John Travolta look—his hair coiffed straight back, his tan Italian pants, so tight she could see the outline of his briefs, and the open-necked silk shirt. He was turning now, bobbing his head to the music, and she started to giggle again. He was sexy, she supposed, but he looked to her like a clone . . . the kind you read about in the *Post*. There was nothing about him that turned her on. He was simply a product of the media. Jesus, it seemed the whole world was getting that way.

She turned away from him in disgust and thought of Peter. He would laugh at her sitting here, slurping this drink, staring at the bottles behind the bar like they were old friends. But she couldn't sleep . . . she couldn't bear to spend another night in her bed, knowing she could be with him. She looked at her watch . . . two thirty. Then she got up and almost slipped at the bar, caught herself, and wandered to the back booth, shutting the door and

161

getting a dime from her purse. She dialed his number slowly, thickly, and felt dizzy, the cheap flat tonic water coming up in her throat. There was a long wait and then the phone rang, and she felt herself tighten up—she was going to make a goddamned fool of herself again. She thought of the consciousness-raising sessions she had attended in Rochester, how brave she had felt then ... without a man to lean on for the first time in years. She had been strong, good, and felt the heroine in her coming alive, which is why she risked coming to New York. But now that she was in love again (and there was no doubt about it), she was weak, thin, barely human. She felt a sudden savage urge to slam the phone down and cancel out on the whole damned thing, but there was that room, the huge, empty bed waiting for her, and she thought of the vastness of the sheets, the terror of their crisp whiteness ... lying there night after night was almost like death. Last night she had dreamed the bed was closing in on her. Oh, Christ, it was ridiculous.

He didn't answer. He wasn't home. But where could he be? Out with another woman? No ... don't start that. She hung up and started out of the booth. The Travolta clone was moving toward her. The Bee Gee's were still playing, and the idiot was even strutting like he was in the damned movie.

"Hey," he said, "like, don't I know you?"

"Buzz off," Debby said. "I don't dig guys."

He moved away, holding his hands up, and she walked by him, tossing her head and pretending to chew gum. It relieved her tension, putting him down—it felt good.

Outside on the street, she looked up at the moon, cursed softly, and hurried down the block. All the way back to her apartment house, she could feel the huge yellow eye staring down at her, the bright rays lancing her back.

162

23

"Harry's disappeared," Beauregard said, not for the first time. He paced up and down in front of the big double bed, rubbing his hand over his muscular chest. Propped up on a pillow, Heather watched him, enjoyed his catlike pacings back and forth across the room. She noticed the way his back curved, how flat his stomach still was... how trim his hips. She wondered how she could have ever stopped noticing before she had left for Paris.

"It's unbelievable," Beauregard said. "They just let him go. I gave Lombardi hell. He should have at least kept him there on some pretext. Christ knows where he is."

He reached down to the blue quilt and picked up his black silk pajama top and put it on. Then he looked down at Heather, who was smiling at him.

"I don't know," she said, putting her copy of *The Magus* down. "It doesn't make a lot of sense to me. If he *had* committed the murders, he would never have gone down to talk with you and Lombardi without a lawyer."

"Yeah," Beauregard said, "unless he was supremely confident he could pull it off."

"Right," Heather said. "Did he seem supremely confident?"

"No."

"And on top of that, trying to run out . . . that doesn't make much more sense either. It only makes him look worse. He must know they are going to catch him."

Beauregard nodded and leaned back so that his shoulders and head rested on Heather's legs.

"I know," he said. "It doesn't make any sense at all. Nothing does."

Suddenly, he tensed up and pounded his fist into his palm.

"Beau," Heather said, "it's not your fault those patients died."

"It's not acceptable," Beauregard said. "Unnecessary deaths are unacceptable, and this . . . I've worked my ass off to make that place the best . . . so many of us have. And it's all being undone by some goddamned crazy force. It's enough to make me sick."

She looked at him with alarm. She had seen him like this only twice before . . . When two patients had died in spite of all he had tried to do.

There had been that girl, Kathy, who had leukemia . . . just a teen-ager, and Beau had been a resident. She had been so very sick, so very, very sick, and Beau had become friends with her . . . lost his distance from the case. He hadn't slept for months, worrying about her . . . the long talks about the unfairness of it, the absurdity of his job. In the end she had died, and Beau had been crushed, but finally he had seemed relieved.

Then there had been the old man, Mr. Robinson. He had so many things wrong with him that he had become the subject of black humor among the staff—they called him a walking plague—but Beau had not found it funny. He had talked to him, learned of his life in the Bronx, his candy store, his children, his courage in the war, and she remembered Beau going through agonizing sleepless nights, staring out the windows at the gas lamp, going

164

over the old man's life again and again. And finally Robinson had died too, right on the operating table, and Beau had been frantic, upset, and even visited his grave. Since those days, though, he had become a complete professional, keeping his distance from the patients. Until this—this thing had gotten to him.

"Is there anything else, Beau?" Heather asked.

"Oh yeah . . . there's quite a few things. Like Peter Cross. I saw him today at the hospital. I started to say something to him and he looked startled, like I was going to jump down his throat. And when I mentioned Harry to him, he got very nervous and then he put his hand up to this scratch on his cheek. I asked him about that and he said he cut himself shaving. That was very strange. Then I saw Debby . . . and she seemed uptight too. Very antsy . . . couldn't talk to me at all."

"Oh," said Heather, "that's odd—I was just wondering about Debby. Wondering if she took my advice. She called the other day—said she and Peter hadn't been getting along. He seemed mad at her."

"So they've had a fight? I wonder if she gave him the scratch?"

Heather ran her long fingers through Beauregard's black hair.

"That's entirely possible," she said. "I remember some of our early battles. They do tend to be pretty rough."

"Yes," Beauregard said, "especially when one of the parties is a little weird . . . when he lives in his head to the exclusion of everything else."

"Peter?" Heather said. "Aren't you being a little unfair."

"Maybe," Beauregard said. "I was just thinking out loud. Peter has changed toward us . . . and Harry is missing . . . does any of that add up?"

Now Heather sat straight up in bed.

"Beau?" she said. "I'm surprised at you. This, if you'll pardon me for saying so, darling, sounds like the true old conservative Beauregard of yesteryear."

Beauregard laughed nervously and sipped his wine.

"Even if I told you that Harry Gardner thinks Peter framed him?"

She gasped.

"You didn't tell me," she said.

"I'm not allowed to tell anybody. But that's what was said down at the police station."

Suddenly the phone rang, and both of them jumped as though they had been pierced by a needle.

Beauregard picked it up.

"Lombardi," he said. "What gives me the honor?"

"Be kind," the nasal voice said. "I've had a rough day. They were going to make me technical advisor on a new cop series called Stark, but the networks axed it. It was a very severe blow to my self-esteem."

"Are you calling for grief counseling?" Beauregard said.

"No," Lombardi said, "but that's a good line. I might work that into my new script. You really ought to read it. It's about a series of murders at a large New York hospital. The police think they have the killer, but he jumps. They comb the city for him, break down doors, and look under the subway. Then we switch to a close-up of the pier around Twelfth Street. We find a body drifting up, his head all bashed in, maybe from where he fell, but more likely from a blunt object."

"Gardner?" Beauregard said. "You found Harry?"

"That's not all," Lombardi said. "Whoever did this was pretty good with a needle. He's been shot with something. I think we got to talk to some of your people—starting with Dr. Cross."

"Talk to Peter?" Beauregard said.

"You got any better ideas?" Lombardi said. "If so, turn

them over. The boys at the studio are licking their chops. This could be big, real big."

"Where are you now?" Beauregard said.

"Not Twenty-One," Lombardi said. He read Beau the number.

"Stay there," Beauregard said.

He hung up the phone.

24

Two doctors and an attendant waited for the ambulance as it entered the emergency gate. The siren screamed across the roofs of Eastern, and the red light whirled frantically as the driver pulled to a screeching halt. The attendants wasted no time getting the doors open and pulled out the stretcher bearing the young woman. She looked at them, frightened, her eyes wide open in fear, and when one of them went to hold her hand, she grabbed his so powerfully that he could not get away from her.

"It's going to be all right, miss," he said. "It's going to be just fine. Don't worry . . . everything is going to be just fine."

She began to cry, her tears running down her face, spoiling her makeup, wetting the roots of her red hair.

"Jesus," she said, "I feel so damned afraid. I'm sorry. I can't believe this is happening to me."

The attendant, a tall boy named Gerald who looked more like a basketball player than a med student, tried a smile. But he looked so unconvincing that she began to panic and started to cry louder.

Quickly they got her through the doors and began wheeling her down the hall. As they did, she sobbed loudly and then groaned.

Peter Cross came out of the canteen, where he was sitting, drinking some grapefruit juice. He saw her go by, saw her pale red face, the pain in her eyes.

He spied one of the attendants.

"Hey, Garrison, who's the girl?"

"Good-looking," Garrison said. He smiled a bit and shuffled his feet, which pointed in opposite directions. He was a dull boy from Arkansas and liked nothing better than racing home after he got off and playing his entire collection of Patsy Cline albums.

"Yeah," Cross said. "Very attractive."

"She's a dancer, named Martha Boston," Garrison said. "Modern dancer . . . with the Joffrey. Or to be technically correct, I should say, 'was' a dancer. She's had some kind of stroke and her entire left side is paralyzed. They're going to have to operate on her in the morning."

"Is that right?" Cross said.

In his stomach he heard a rumbling so loud that he was surprised the farm boy couldn't hear it as well.

He moved slowly down the dark hallway, feeling as though at last he had arrived somewhere, that he had been dreaming all his life and knew it, but now, at long last, he had managed to part the curtain and walk through the other side . . . no longer was he a dreamer but the dream itself. This was all his, the white walls, the patients, the nurses looking like nuns. They were all his, to do with as he would. He came upon her lying with her eyes closed.

"Hello," he said softly, ever so softly, for he felt at that moment so compassionate, so in touch with her, that no words needed to be spoken at all.

"Hello," she said waking and smiling at him.

The red hair, the fullness of her breasts, the absurdity

of it. He wanted to laugh out loud . . . not at her, but at the common stupidity of it all. If there was a God, he would spit in his eye.

He moved to the end of her bed and picked up her chart, pretended to check her blood pressure and the other details. Again he wanted to laugh, simply tell her there was no reason to worry, none at all, for everything that really mattered had already been decided. The chart with its "vital signs," the hospital with its oxygen tents, its laser beams, its sophisticated gases, its knives, its smug golf-playing suburban doctors . . . all of that was history now.

"How do you feel?" he said. "How are you?"

"I don't know," she said. Then a tear came down her cheek, and she put her hand up to her face.

"They say I may be paralyzed for life," she said. "I'm a dancer . . . I can't afford that."

He moved around to her side of the bed.

"No," he said, sitting down on the chair next to her. "No, of course you can't. You dance . . . Tell me how do you feel . . . dancing?"

"It's wonderful," she said, moving her head toward him, the tears still coming.

"Your body feels wonderful?" he said.

"Yes," she said. "Sometimes when you are really there . . . it's almost as if . . ."

He put his finger over her lips.

"It's almost as if you don't have a body."

"Yes," she said. "How did you know?"

"I know about those kinds of things," he said. "It's my business to know. I'm a doctor."

"Yes," she said. "But now. Oh, God, I can't believe this is happening to me."

He sat down on the chair next to her bed. He took a deep breath and smelled her perfume. He felt light-

170

headed, as though he could float away.

"It's going to be all right," he said, offering her a handkerchief. "It's going to be all right. Where are you from?"

"Philadelphia," she said. "I'd been in this town for a year. I couldn't get any work. Then I got this part in 'Romeo and Juliet' and I got to sign on with the Joffrey. It was going to be my big moment. Oh, shit . . ."

He looked at her with total compassion. The tricks the body could play. If people had any real sense they would never feel safe. Never.

"You shouldn't be upset," he said. "It's going to be fine . . . There's an operation that is almost 100 percent sure. I'll make sure I'm your anesthesiologist. I'm on tomorrow. Trust in me, and the other doctors, and try to sleep. That's just what you need. A nice, long sleep."

"Yes," she said. "I know it. Oh, God. I'm so scared."

She reached out and grabbed his hand, and he took hers and felt her soul pass from her own body to his. He wanted to bare his teeth, to howl, but he merely smiled.

"I'll check in with you before the operation," he said to her. "Sleep . . . just sleep."

25

Beefy Sloan sat in his battered pale blue Pinto beneath a dying elm in front of Sig's Bar and Grill. In his huge hands were a pair of binoculars, which had been splattered with red paint by his five-year-old son who had been trying to help him redecorate their old house in Queens. Beefy was looking at the Doc's house, waiting for some movement, but all that ever happened was an occasional shadow on the lime green curtains. Beefy didn't understand what the point of it was anyway... they already had the other guy, the muscleman. He'd like to see that jerk's corpse after the lab boys got done with it. So what was Lombardi doing putting him down on this case... watching this other guy. It was chilly out... and worse, it was boring. Beefy longed to be slouched in a booth at the Sage Diner, hoisting a few with Ding Dong Delbert and the others... maybe watching the Knicks on TV. Though the Knicks wasn't as good as they used to be on account of the whole team was made up of Jiggs.

He picked up the glasses again and waited. Goddamn, it was boring here. He looked over at Sig's. Through the open window he could see two guys jawing and drinking down Miller's. Jesus! It was obvious nothing was going

172

to happen. Ninety-nine times out of a hundred on stake-
out you came up with nothing. Fuck it! He put down
the glasses and got out of the car.

He walked through his living room, looked up at his
Hopper painting, "Rooms by the Sea." He had always
liked that painting, always cherished it . . . a room opening into blue water, no steps . . . just like stepping into
the wakefulness of a dream. Which is how he felt when
he killed them. As though he had completed a picture of
his own, the outline of which was traced faintly in his
mind the night before. It was like a performance that
any great artist could understand. Certainly, a great
musician, or even an athlete. He had read accounts of
athletes imagining themselves running the 440 in record
time, and then going out the next day and doing it, and
when it was done, they said they felt they had simply
acted out their dream. The problem was, of course, they
dreamed so pathetically small. They understood nothing
of the alleviation of human misery, of the higher calling of
the spirit. They were tied irrevocably to the petty, the
banal, the whole boatload of stupid, trivial earthly cares.

He walked over to his brown bag, unzipped it, and
pulled out the needles. He transferred the potassium into
one syringe. He held it up in his hand. So small, so clean.
It was like a delicately carved work of art, and he thought
it more beautiful than any sculpture; it made more sense.
And better yet, it was utterly disposable. The end product
of a shit-heap civilization with its taco stands, burger
kings, insults to the beauty of the human spirit. Yes, and
practical . . . not merely decorative. It worked. It did the
job. As Martha Boston would find out tomorrow morning. He thought of her there, waiting for him, her face
ringed by red. She looked like she was on fire . . . and he
would be there soon to put it out.

173

The doorbell rang, and he jumped . . . placed the needles back into their case and jammed the empty potassium bottle into the case.

"Who is it?" he said, trying to sound calm.

"Peter, it's me . . . Debby."

"Debby?"

His breath was taken away, and he wanted to turn and run . . . yet she was there . . . he had missed her so . . .

"Peter, let me in. Really . . . I've got to see you."

"All right," he said, though he wanted to say, "No, get away."

He moved toward the door and opened it. She was there, her blond hair frizzed out in a million curls, her green eyes and impossibly perfect mouth. He wanted to stop it before it got out of hand, but it was too late; she was in his arms, holding him.

"Peter," she said, "Peter, I've missed you."

"Me too . . . God, Debby, you feel good."

He kissed her deeply and felt her tongue in his mouth, and suddenly he felt that he might cry. He pulled away from her, held her by the shoulders.

"I'm sorry about the fight," he said. "God, that was silly of me."

"It's all right," she said. "All that matters is that we're together again. Really."

"Yes," he said. "Of course."

Then he kissed her again, and he felt as though what she had said was true. For those few moments all the rest was gone, and he felt a perfect peace.

"Listen," she said, holding him and walking him to the couch. "I've been thinking . . . Both of us are over-wrought. You know? It's really true. We need to get away from the hospital . . . from the city all together . . . this damned place gets so crazy."

"That would be nice, Debby, but . . ."

174

"No buts," she said, sitting down next to him and hugging him tightly. "My uncle has a place up the Hudson. It's a wonderful old cabin. I used to go there as a little girl. We can stay there, sit out on the screen porch and just relax. It will be wonderful."

"But, Debby . . ."

She kissed his ear and ran her hand across his leg.

"It's all set anyway," she said. "I know you have to work. Oh, Peter don't be mad . . . I called Chung and asked him to take your place. He said he'd be happy to. He's getting ready to go in . . . tomorrow morning."

He thought of Martha Boston, sitting there waiting for him, and he felt a panic, but Debby was holding onto him tightly and kissing him and whispering his name, and he felt fulfilled, strangely fulfilled, and that scared him as well. But, God, it felt good . . . Besides, there was plenty of time for Martha . . . After her operation. It would even be safer then. Certainly, if he had tried anything during the operation he might have been caught. Yes, maybe Debby coming was his salvation. He had to plan carefully. There could never be any mistakes. Quickly, he turned and kissed her on the nose.

"Yes," he said. "Yes . . . I want to go with you. When do we leave?"

"Right now," Debby said. "Right now."

She laughed and ran across the apartment and opened the front door. On the landing in the hall was her overnight bag.

"Pretty sure of yourself," he said.

She smiled at him, picked up the bag, and brought it in.

"Start packing, Peter," she said.

Beefy Sloan staggered out of Sig's Bar and Grill, his head feeling like the Goodyear Blimp. Those five quick bullshots had done the job. Not quite the man he used to be up in Queens. He shoulda eaten his lunch, but lately his favorite bar had been changing their meats . . . serving stuff that tasted like Spam, and he was too much a man of habit to find a new one. Now he started across the street, his car hazy and warm-looking in the late afternoon haze.

Suddenly, he looked down the street, and there in front of him, walking toward his car was the Doc and some girl. He couldn't believe it. He started for his car, realized that he was parked facing the wrong direction. Quickly he ran to the door, leaped in, smashing his head on the Pinto roof. Shit, they were getting away. He turned and looked back and saw the girl getting into the car, but the Doc was standing there staring at him. Oh, shit, maybe the guy spotted him. He had been nosing around the hospital . . . If he had, he might not go back to the goddamned room and fall for the game they were playing. Jesus, he thought of reporting that to Lombardi . . . It was impossible . . . He'd kill him, eat him for dinner, cut off his balls and hang them from the World Trade Center.

Beefy looked in the rear-view. The Doc and the broad were pulling away . . . Nah, he hadn't spotted him . . . They were just going for a drive . . . Maybe for fucking dinner, right? It was dinner fucking time, right? Sure . . . It was all right . . . He'd tail them . . . Yeah, they thought they could get away from old Beefy, but there was no way . . . no way at all. Quickly he gunned the little car forward and then started a tight U in the narrow street. A woman with a Gristede's shopping bag was coming up the block, and he was aiming right at her. "Out of the way, bitch," he mumbled under his breath. The woman threw up her arms and dropped her groceries on the

176

ground, then fell down amid them. Beefy laughed to himself, a deep, piglike moan which came from the back of his throat. Then the laugh turned into a belch, and the belch into a curse. "Fucking broads," he said to himself, "always fuck you up. The world would be a whole lot better wifout 'em." He made the run and started down the street, two blocks behind Peter Cross.

They drove in his Mercedes up the West Side Highway, Debby chatting amiably about the glories of the countryside, but Cross could scarcely hear. Reflected in the sinking sun behind him was the battered Pinto with the huge-jowled man behind the wheel. His face looked like a piece of raw fish, and Cross knew that he had seen the face somewhere before ... the hospital ... he was sure of it. And the guy was not a patient ... no way. No, he was a cop ... He had been with Detective Lombardi the day they had come to take away Harry. IIe stepped hard on the gas, and the car shot ahead of the Pinto like a pinball.

"Peter," Debby said, "aren't we traveling a little fast? I know you're tense, but the whole idea of this trip is for the two of us to relax."

He looked over at her and smiled, then reached across and stroked her cheek.

"I like to drive fast," he said. "It relaxes me."

She took his hand and rubbed it on her cheek, then kissed his fingers. He felt the tip of her tongue, and the wetness of it traveled through his arm, to his brain, heart, and lungs. He took a deep breath.

"Debby." He felt himself get hard. His thighs trembled a bit, and he left his hand there, so she might kiss it again.

In the rear-view he saw the Pinto moving up behind him once again.

"Jesus," Beefy said out loud.

He had brought out his binoculars and was busy zooming in on the Doc. He couldn't believe his eyes. The Doc was getting his fingers sucked by that chick. These Jap cameras was the real McCoy. You could see even the tip of her tongue, lashing in and out, the way her mouth made a perfect little O . . . Oh, shit, this was too fucking much. The Doc was a car freak. Beefy had seen them kind before, oh, yessir—remembered a guy who could only get it up if he was dressed like a Yankee catcher and his girl an ump. Another one who had to have his room covered with Big Macs, and him dressed like Ronald McDonald—but who woulda figured the Doc. Oh, shit, now he's putting his hand on her breast . . . Jesus, I don't believe it. Beefy looked down at his own crotch and noticed a mighty bulge . . . He shut his eyes and thought of dinosaurs coming out of a primeval ooze.

Then the Mercedes cut to the outside lane, blew a black puff of smoke in his direction, and was quickly five car-lengths away.

"Peter," Debby said, "this is crazy . . . there are cars all around us . . . oh, Peter."

She started to laugh a little self-consciously.

"I can't believe we're acting like this," she said. "This is like something out of a porno flick. But, oh, Christ."

His hand was rubbing her breasts, and his eyes were on the rear-view, watching, waiting for the Pinto to move up. There . . . he's coming . . . yes . . .

He saw the Pinto move out into the left lane, cutting off a Porsche . . . and he held her nipple between his thumb and forefinger. He felt his body jerk a little, as if

178

he had been electrocuted, shocked . . . and he thought this was it, this was what made it all bearable . . . the shocks. Anything less, and you were not quite alive.

Beefy didn't need his glasses anymore. He was right up behind the guy. Christ, he could see her breast . . . He could see her eyes close and her body sink down on the seat.

"What I would give," he said out loud.

He shut his eyes again and thought of his wife's body . . . like a morass of swamp mire . . . shit . . . Then he opened his eyes, ready for more . . . but the Doc was gone.

He stepped on the pedal, cut to the far left lane.

Then he heard the diesel engine blow. Loud and long, like a shrieking mother-in-law on the crab-grass lawn.

"Peter," she said, "oh, Peter, are there any cars around us . . . Jesus . . . I feel like a pervert. I do . . . Christ . . . that feels good . . . oh, shit . . ."

"Debby . . . Debby . . ." he said.

No Space now . . . never any Space . . . as long as you were out of the body, never any Space . . . but full, full, warm all over.

Beefy didn't have time to look. But he heard a sickening shearing sound and saw the truck barreling down on his front side . . . The warm beer shot through his throat, and he screamed out and wheeled the car to the far right. The North Western Van Lines clipped his back fender, bashing it loose . . . Beefy's car was pushed forward as though a giant hand had descended from the sky. He looked to his right and saw the tan Porsche, only a few inches away. The driver had dropped his Glen plaid racing cap, and his eyes and mouth were the same size. Beefy stepped on the gas as the Porsche slammed on the brakes, and the Pinto went skidding across the last right-hand lane, hit the macadam doing ninety-five, and went off a four-foot curved shoulder, across a rocky field toward a huge gas tank which lay fifty feet away.

"Agggghhhhhhhh," Beefy screamed. "Aghhhhhh."

He was aware that he sounded like Deputy Dog on TV, but after the scream a curious thing happened. He simply assumed that it was all over. He began to relax. The car rolled forward, faster and faster. Beefy held tight to the wheel and began to hum "Mother Macree."

"Jesus, look!" Debby said. "There's been an accident. That man is headed for the gas tank over there . . . I don't think he is going to be able to stop . . ."

"No?" said Peter, rubbing his hand on her thigh.

"No," said Debby. "Jesus . . . Oh, Jesus . . . that feels good . . . Peter . . . we shouldn't . . . It's going to be horrible. Oh, Christ."

The Pinto rolled faster and faster. Beefy Sloan began to scream about ten yards away from the huge Beta Oil sign. He hit the brakes and felt his foot go through the floorboards . . . Then he shut his eyes and started to cry.

His car hit the chain-link screen and knocked it down as though it were a loose front tooth. Beefy heard the sickening crumble of wire, saw the gas tank come closer, and held on.

One foot away from the tank, the Pinto's brakes decided to work. The car stopped as neatly as though it were pulling into a Jack-in-the-Box. Beefy could hear the sound of his heartbeat reverberating through the front seat. It was so loud that for a second he thought his radio was on, and he reached down to turn it off. Then he looked up at the Beta Boy, a huge dark blue drop of oil with long curling lashes and a killer grin.

180

Big red letters hung over Beefy's brow.

Better Try Beta.

"You bet your ass," Beefy said. "You bet your ass."

He got out of the car and looked down at his pants. They were dark, and when he looked back up at the sign, he thought he saw it wink.

26

Dr. Oscar Chung felt as fine as any day in his entire life. He whistled Barry Manilow all the way to the hospital, skipped down the hall like a kid racing down the block to buy Marvel Comics, and changed into his OR greens with the enthusiasm of a first-year man. Things were going right for him...he had a girlfriend named Wanda Latowski, they were going bowling later that night, and he was going to be friends with the mysterious Peter Cross.

He wished he'd done a favor for Cross a long time ago, for he had always been attracted to him. Indeed, among the other anesthesiologists, Cross had attained, without his knowledge of course, something of a star status. He was brilliant, aloof, and sometimes wore capes. By comparison the others were all pikers. Chung knew Cross was interested in philosophy. Perhaps they would read the I Ching together. Chung practiced it regularly but told nobody. Doctors were supposed to be rational. But not Cross. He held his individuality aloft, as if it were a banner. Now Chung walked down the hall, his drugs in his Moroccan bag, and headed for Martha Boston's room. It was going to be all right. He and Cross would be pals.

He nodded to a nurse and entered the room. The red-haired woman looked at him and seemed disturbed.

"Who are you?" she said.

"I am Chung," said Chung. "Dr. Chung, your anesthesiologist."

"Dr. Chung?" the woman said nervously. "But I was supposed to see Dr. Cross."

"Alas," Chung said, "he has gone away . . . with his girlfriend to have a vacation. You don't have to worry though, you're in good hands."

"That's why she's worried," said a voice.

Chung gave a small gasp of surprise as Dr. Robert Beauregard and Detective Lombardi walked out of the adjoining room. Behind them Chung thought he saw another man with a camera.

"Is this some kind of surprise?" Chung said. "I love surprises."

"Yeah," Lombardi said. "This is a surprise. Believe that, pal."

The redhead in the bed sat up and got out of the bed. Chung looked at her long, beautiful legs. When she stepped out to the floor, he half expected her to fall.

"It's all right, Chung," she said. "These gams are fine."

She looked up at Beauregard, who had slumped down in his chair. "Now what?"

This had been an acting job Lynne Carter hadn't had to audition for.

"I don't know, Lynne," Beauregard said. "I really don't know."

27

"This is it," Debby said as she got out of the car. She ran up in the bright beams of the lights and raised her arms as if she were giving thanks. Cross smiled, picked up his sports coat off the seat, and got out of the car.

"Isn't it terrific," she said. "God, after what we've been through, we really deserve this."

Cross smiled at her and looked up at the cabin. The screened-in porch looked like something from a New England painting. There were rockers, a card table, and a stuffed owl. The owl's yellow eyes reflected the car lights.

Debby turned and pointed back behind the car.

"Hear the water?" she said. "Down the steps there, is the Hudson. It's perfect. In the morning, Doctor, I will let you take the patient on a walk."

"Why not tonight?" he said, moving forward and slipping his coat over her shoulders. He pulled her to him and kissed her deeply.

"Why not indeed?" she said.

"Come on," she said, smiling at him and racing up the steps onto the porch, and through it to the front door.

He laughed as he watched her long, shapely legs sticking out from under his old tweed jacket. She looked like a happy young kid.

Inside, he immediately smelled the odor of camphor balls and disinfectant. The sick room smells he associated with Lila Lee's rooms. He felt dizzy and began to break out in a sweat. She was somewhere in front of him in the darkness, and he tried finding her but tripped over a chair.

"I'm over here," came the small, disembodied voice.

"Where?"

"Here."

She lit a gas lamp, and then she appeared before him, her shadow great behind her.

She held onto the sleeves of his coat, a silent movie character, and did a short, comical shadow dance for him.

He smiled and felt a rush of affection for her.

"Come here, Debby," he said.

"Oh, no, sir," she said. "You wouldn't take advantage of a poor sick patient, would you?"

"That's not so funny, Debby," he said.

"What?" she laughed. "You're offended? The sex king of the freeway."

"Don't kid me," he said.

He moved closer, but she dodged out of his way, laughing wildly, and then raced to the steps.

"Come up here," she said. "I want to show you my thermometers."

She laughed again and took the steps like a kid, two at a time. He followed her, still confused, suddenly afraid of the dark.

At the top of the steps he smelled it again. Something like the odor of licorice, and he thought of Lila Lee's face all eaten away, the mouth collapsing like a broken trapdoor.

"God, it's musty up here," she said from the dark room.

Then she turned on another lamp and stood in front of him, his oversized coat hanging off her. He looked at her legs and saw she had let her Levis fall to the ground.

"Peter," she said. "Come here . . ."

He moved toward her in the flickering light, took her roughly and kissed her hard, his right hand moving to her ass.

"Debby," he said, "Debby . . ."

She fell backward on the bed, and he landed on her and kissed her again, and then she rolled over and sat on top of him.

"This is what we've both needed," she said. "Christ, just to get away."

He smiled at her, and she took off his sports coat, slowly, sensuously.

"I like this coat," she said. "I like it when you wear it, and I like it on me. It scratches me a little, and I think of you."

She held it up in front of him, then smiled at him and waved it back and forth like a stripper playing with her G-string.

He started to smile, then he remembered something, and the fear came fast, too fast . . .

"Debby," he said, "don't do that."

She looked confused.

"Don't do what?" she said.

"Give me the coat," he said suddenly.

He grasped at it, getting up and knocking her back. Thinking he was joking, she tried to keep it away from him, but as she fell, the coat went sailing out of her hands and landed on the floor behind them. Something fell out of the pocket, and he tried to get down on the floor to retrieve it, but she moved quickly and grabbed it.

"Peter," she said, "what is it?"

Quickly he tried to regain his composure.

"Nothing," he said. "I was just joking."

Then she opened her hand and looked down at the bottle of norepinephrine.

He smiled weakly:

"Debby," he said, "give it to me."

"Peter . . . this bottle . . . why were you so upset?"

Then it hit her. She gasped a little and looked at him, and from the way he was twitching, the pathetic little smile on his face, she knew.

"Peter," she said. "Oh, Jesus . . . Oh, no, no . . . no . . . not you."

He reached down and grabbed her hand, and she opened it slowly, handing him the bottle.

Of course—my coat. I forgot which coat I was wearing. Before I switched all the bottles to my lab coat, I had them in this one and I forgot one.

She fell on her knees in front of him shocked into silence, afraid to look into his face. She felt her fingers, then her whole arm, grow cold, and she wanted to scream but there was no air in the room and she began to gasp. She felt his hand come down, cup her chin, slowly raise her head toward him.

"I love you," he said.

"And I you," she said, without hesitation.

Then she reached up and took him around the neck and kissed him hard, and he was amazed. He had assumed she would be mad . . . that she would want to turn him in, but she was kissing him. More passionately than before. She loved him for it. Oh, God, he was so lucky . . . so very lucky . . . and he pulled her up to him . . . shutting his eyes, thankful for the chance to finally tell someone his wonderful secret . . . to share it with a woman he loved.

"Oh, Debby," he said.

Then something terribly hot burned the back of his

neck and he screamed, and fell back on the bed. For a
few seconds the pain was so terrible that he couldn't
move and he heard her scream and saw her run out of the
room. Then he turned and saw what she had done. The
oil lamp on the nearby end table. She had brought it
down on his head. He picked it up and heaved it against
the window, watched it fall and shatter . . . saw the flames
lick at the old gauzy curtains. Then he got up, screamed
at her. And went to the top of the stairs. She was already out the front door, before he started down.

"Beefy blew it." Lombardi said. He dusted off his
key-lime Georgio Armani sports jacket, and sighed.

Beauregard looked at him. Then he turned and looked
down at Yvonne.

"How the hell did this happen?" he said.

"I don't know," she said. "It's the one thing we didn't
count on . . . *Debby* . . . She called Chung and got him
to take Peter's place."

"I know," Beauregard said. "I know all about it."

Across the room Chung stared at everyone and smiled.
Lombardi looked at him and smiled back like someone
had put a pin in his stomach.

"What's all the fuss?" Chung said. "I covered for
Peter. Why is everyone upset?"

"Fucking Beefy." Lombardi shook his head, paced to
and fro. 'If he hadn'ta blown it, we'd have Cross in the
crapper right now. He lucked out."

Beauregard walked over to his desk and sat down in
the chair like he was a bag of bowling balls.

"I can't believe it," he said. "Where the hell could
they have gone? Look, Yvonne, I want you to call
Debby's father for me upstate. Find out if she is up
there, and if not, if they have any other place . . . a sum-

188

mer place. Call any girlfriends she has on the nursing staff..."

Yvonne nodded and walked out of the room.

"What a mess," Lombardi said. "If he's taken her somewhere, Jesus...anything could happen..."

He stalked around the room and let his breath out in short, impatient spurts.

"We blew it, Doc... We had him dead if he came in here. Now it's his move. We can't do a thing."

"Debby," Beauregard said.

"I wouldn't think about her too much, Doc," the detective said. "I'd think about whoever comes next..."

Outside he watched as she sat ten yards away from him in the car. The doors were locked, and she looked ludicrous sitting there, naked. He felt embarrassed for her, really.

"You might as well come back in, Debby," he said laconically. "You can't go anywhere...I've got the keys."

She started to scream then, and he looked around sheepishly.

"Don't make a scene," he said.

He started moving toward the car slowly. If he was careful, acted normal, perhaps she would see...Perhaps he had been wrong about her. No one had come to arrest him, so she hadn't known. That was a point in her favor. Definitely... Now, if he could just make it clear what he had been up to, she would see... Except his back... his back... it was burning, a charred piece of meat. The fucking cunt. The worthless scumbag cunt...

"Come out of there," he said. "Come out now. I'm serious."

She came out then, but not as he wished. She opened

the door and ran as fast as she could toward the steps which led down to the shore. Before he could make a move, she had disappeared over the hill.

He moved toward her quickly, stopped by the car, and got out his potassium-filled syringe. He had been planning to use it on Martha Boston, but this was better, this was much better...

Now he took it and headed down the long narrow white steps which gleamed like a row of false teeth... Around him was honeysuckle, and he realized that was what he had been smelling all along.

"Debby," he said, holding the syringe tightly. "Debby, come back... Debby... We can talk about this..."

But she wasn't talking. She was nearly at the bottom of the steps.

He ran down the steps quickly... saw her turn right down the beach, and then he became scared. There were lights several hundred yards away. More homes. If she made it to one of them, he would never be able to explain to her. She mustn't run away from him.

"Debby," he said, laughing a little, and sounding like he had when he was playing tag in his back alley in Baltimore, "I'm going to catch you... Here I come..."

He began to laugh a little, then a lot. It was funny, really. He was a doctor, a man who helped people, and here he was chasing his crazy girlfriend, and she with just panties on. It was crazy... a burlesque. Why didn't she see how crazy it was.

She was fifty yards ahead of him, but he was in good condition, and he closed in fast. And she was crying and screaming. That was a mistake too. You couldn't run well if you were busy screaming. She should know that. He would tell her when he caught her. Then he would help her. She wouldn't have to scream again. It was going to be fine.

190

"Debby," he said, "Debby, come on . . . Wait."

As he yelled at her, she turned and tripped, falling on the beach. He stepped up his pace, and in a second stood above her. They were both drenched in sweat, panting. . . . She was down on all fours in front of him, and he found himself looking at her as if she were his pet.

"Debby," he said softly, "you ought to get up. I've got to talk to you. It's not like you think."

She looked up at him, saw the syringe, and then she grabbed a rock, and threw it at him with all her strength. It struck him in the cheek, and he felt a flash of pain, then fell back, rubbing his face.

"All right now . . . all right," he said.

He was talking quietly, very quietly, and while he talked he moved forward swiftly, grabbed at her arm, but she scratched his wrist with her nails and picked up another stone.

"I'll take that," he said, holding out his hand. It was like the movies. He was the warden, and she the crazed killer. He'd calm her down.

"Yes, you'll take it," she said. She flung it at him and hit him again, this time on the neck, and he screamed and came toward her. She scrambled to her feet and ran backwards, toward the river, and then she was in it . . . and had been knocked off her feet by the swift current. She started to drift away from him, quickly, too quickly, and he went in after her.

But she had disappeared in a tangle of logs and brush in front of him. He grabbed onto a log and looked to the shore, and for the first time he became really afraid. If she made it back to the shore she might get away. He sucked in his breath, and felt his body becoming numb. The water was cold, very cold. He saw a big rock up ahead, and started for it . . . then he heard something behind him, and he turned, and saw her behind a log and a huge overhanging fern.

"Debby."

But she was already half out of the water, and he began half paddling and pulling himself toward her.

He caught her when she fell into deeper water, and he grabbed her arms.

"Debby," he said, "Debby, you have to listen."

But she wasn't listening. She was screaming now. He was afraid someone would hear. He grabbed her arms and pulled her toward him, but she spat at him and wrenched herself free. She tried to move toward the shore, but he grabbed her again and spun her around, and yet once more she got away, and dove underwater. He started to dive with her, but instead he waited. . . . The water was so cold, she couldn't stay down there long . . . and as he had expected, she came up . . . only a few feet away from him, downstream a bit, and he started toward her.

She was screaming now, "Help me, help me," and he moved toward her quickly. She was crying and waving, and he grabbed her head and began holding her under . . . but she was stronger than he had anticipated. She kicked and struggled so that he had to increase his grip on her neck. He hadn't wanted to do that. Hurt her. . . .

It was then he heard the motor, and when he looked he saw a boat coming toward them, and a spotlight.

"Hey," a man's voice called, "hey what's going on over there?"

He felt her grow limp under the water, and he knew that he had her. She was through—drowned or frozen— and he had no more time. Quickly he gasped in air and dove underwater, pulling her with him. He looked at her, head down, for a silent moment, then he let go of her neck and watched the current carry her downstream.

He heard the sound of the motorboat coming closer, and he swam toward the rocks and the logs, surfacing between them, and watched as the boat-light passed just over his head. Then he scrambled toward the shore. When he reached the land he fell down on his knees and gasped for air. He was trembling, shaking, and he felt a terrible, sickening sorrow. Before he could think about it, even before he could feel the hollow space fill up, as it always did (but would it, even if it was the woman he loved?), he smelled smoke, and he saw that on the hill the house was burning. He could hear the wood crackling, see the bright orange flames coming from the woods like the yellow locks of a woman's hair.

"Good-bye, Debby," he said softly.

Then he hurried up the hill, toward the car.

28

He parked his car in front of the East Side brownstone, and checked his face in the mirror. He had stopped at a Howard Johnson's on the road and was all cleaned up except for the scratch across his forehead. She was a strong bitch—no question. For a moment he was sad, but it turned quickly to rage.

He squinted out into the morning sunlight with a vast hatred at the neatly tended flowerboxes with the season's first tulips coming through the soil, at the fine oaken doors with the big brass knocker, at the Edwardian curtains, the wide, handsome latticed windows.

It was all here, everything he had never had, everything he had stood against. The incredible plush softness of it all, the cozy creature comfort, the polite hello, the gentle good-bye, see you later, darling . . . The cozy old sow of a housemaid, the perfectly divine wife, with her illusion of depth, her facile, banal chatter . . . all of it only chatter, for her bottom line was the material world, the things she could own. And one must not forget the darling daughter, so wise for her age, so full of herself and her vast ego. Soon she would be hopping off to Vassar or Sarah Lawrence to take her place among other little rich boys and girls.

Yes, soon, soon. But before she left, he was going to

pay them all a visit, one they wouldn't soon forget. He
would leave his mark on them, on each of them, and they
would know that they owned nothing, they would know,
as he did, that each and every one of us were men from
the dark side of the moon.

He clutched the needles in his hand and took from his
bag two bottles of potassium and a Demerol-Valium solution. A little appetizer before dinner, dear?

Now the problem was how to get in the place, how
best to get to Beauregard. He checked his watch. Yes, it
was only seven thirty. Beauregard would be out soon.
Should he just attack him on the street? That was dan-
gerous, for Beauregard was strong. Perhaps if he followed
him to the hospital . . . Yes, somewhere along the way . . .

Suddenly the door opened. He ducked down, then told
himself to relax. They don't suspect you. He straightened
up and saw Mrs. O'Shea pat Sarah on the head. She
handed Sarah her bookbag, and then kissed her on the
nose, and shut the door. Sarah went down the steps,
stopped to admire the tulips, and started down the street.

Cross started the engine and drove the car slowly behind her. When she came to the traffic light, he pulled
up beside her and honked the horn.

"Hey," he said cheerfully, "want a ride?"

At first she wouldn't look at him, and he started to
panic. But he tried again.

"Sarah . . . it's me . . . Peter Cross. How you doing?"

This time she turned toward him, her face still frozen,
on guard.

"Peter," she said, breaking into a smile. "What on
earth happened to your face?"

He checked himself in the mirror. Christ, he should
have thought of that.

"Actually, that's why I came by," he said. "To see your
dad. We had a terrible time at the hospital last night . . .

A patient went nuts and tried to kill me . . . Drug reaction
. . . Whew . . . I'm lucky it isn't worse."

She came closer to the car door.

"Dad's not home just now," Sarah said. "He's at the
hospital on some kind of emergency, I think."

"You're kidding?" Peter said. "And I was just there
and never thought to page him. Oh, well, I'll have to go
back. Meanwhile, can I give you a lift to school?"

She smiled at him, and he felt the Space opening.

"I'm never supposed to accept rides from strangers,"
she said.

He smiled at her and opened the door.

"But since you've already had such a rough night," she
said, "maybe I can make an exception."

He pushed the door open for her, and she scrambled
inside.

Down the block Mrs. O'Shea opened the door of the
house and looked down the street. Sarah had forgotten
her notes for her science project . . . That child . . . She
looked down the block and saw Sarah get into the Mercedes, and she started to cry out after her, but then the
door was closed and Sarah was gone.

Long after she had heard him call her name, she had
floated in the water, though its coldness was like a scalpel
on her arms, legs, hands. Now, certain that he was gone,
she raised up her head and ran her freezing fingers around
her raw and aching throat. Above her, on the hill, she
could hear the sound of fire engines and the screams of
men. "Bring a hose around here . . . Too late . . . Forget
it . . ."

She thought of the summers she had spent in the
house, and she suddenly started to cry. The house had
burned down, nothing left of it . . . nothing left of her,
either. Oh, God, it was so awful. Then she got hold of

herself and started moving toward the shore.

"A hundred yards to go," she said, "just a hundred yards."

She lost her balance for a moment, then slowly she regained her footing and went forward . . . step by step, gaining on the shore. Then she was there, somehow at the bottom of the steps, and she realized the tide had washed her down to them. The fire was brighter now, and hotter; she started up the stairs, but her feet were asleep, filled with needles—needles like the ones he had used—and she started to spin madly, tried to hold onto the rail, but fell down the white wooden steps, while above her a huge figure with a bright red face looked down.

"My God," said Beauregard. "Where could he have taken her?"

He sat at a long table in the conference room. Lombardi sat across from him and squinted through watery eyes.

"We've got his place staked," he said. "We've got two hundred men on the streets. All the main bridges have been cordoned off. There's no way he can get out of town."

"Which only leaves him about a million other places in town," Beauregard said. He had begun to feel sick . . . terribly sick . . . Sarah . . . My God, he had no conception . . . None at all . . . Yet he might have been able to stop it.

"We've got to try and figure where he would go," said Jimmy Myers, draining a Tab.

"He's got no friends," Beauregard said. "And we still haven't heard from Debby. He may have . . ."

Beauregard shook his head. He was a man of action; there was no greater pain than to sit helplessly by.

Behind him the door opened, and Heather came in.

"Beau," she said. "He took her right out of the house."

Beauregard got up and went to her. He held her tightly, feeling at once the urge to comfort and to hide his head. He had to be a smart guy . . . work it out on his own.

"Oh, Beau . . ."

"Now take it easy, Heather."

"Take it easy?" she said. "Take it easy? I'll tell you about taking it easy. If that sick bastard does one thing to Sarah . . ."

The phone lit up on Lombardi's desk. Quickly he picked it up.

"Hello . . . On fire? See if you can find the nurse."

Beauregard and Heather turned anxiously toward Lombardi.

"No . . . it wasn't your daughter. They think they have a lead to Debby Hunter. Seems Beefy was able to follow them to a place on the Hudson. It's now up in flames— totalled."

The room was absolutely silent.

"We've got to do something," Beauregard said. "We've got to."

Heather began to cry softly, and Beauregard held her against his shoulder.

"Oh, God," she said. "And I went off and left you both. Oh, God, Beau . . ."

"Don't say that," Beauregard said. "You did what was right. This has nothing to do with that. No matter how this thing turns out . . . you did the right thing."

Two police officers came through the door. They were both breathless.

"Captain," the tall blond one said, "I think we've got something. The suspect's car was just spotted."

"Where?" said Beauregard.

"That's the weird part," said the shorter man. "Not two blocks away from here."

198

"Jesus," said Lynne Carter. "What the hell? . . ."

"Sixty-first and York," said the other cop. "We've got men in every building . . ."

"Yeah," said Lombardi. "Good." But his voice was distant, preoccupied.

He looked up at Beauregard.

"You know what I think," he said.

"He's coming here," Beauregard said. "He's coming here."

Beefy Sloan reached down and picked her up, gently carrying her out in front of him. He moved up the steps gingerly, and she opened her eyes in a second, saw his huge swollen face, and started to cry.

"Who are you?" she said.

"The guy that ran into the oil tanker," he said. "Only I'm still alive. My car needs a little work, though."

"You're a cop?" she said.

"Maybe," Beefy said back. "Maybe I'm a cop."

They walked by the house, and she heard the shouts of the firemen, felt the flames' warmth, and then she asked him to put her down.

"We've got to get to Dr. Beauregard," she said.

"I know, lady," he said. "We got to."

He walked over to his car, the window of which looked like it belonged in church. There were a million cracks, the left tire was nearly flat, and the right headlight was smashed. She leaned on him and shook her head.

"I don't think we're going to make it," she said.

"We're gonna make it," he said. "Count on Beefy. He won't let you down."

Above them they heard a noise, and Beefy Sloan watched as a helicopter landed in the clearing just a hundred yards away from them.

"Here we go, lady," he said.

He dragged her away from the shouting firemen, but she managed to turn once more to stare at her uncle's house, her retreat ... Now it, too, was gone. He was like a disease, a plague. Anything he touched was dead.

"Come on, lady," Beefy said. "We gotta get you to the hospital."

She heard the last word and began to shudder, and then she felt she would buckle. But she thought of Cross, and Beauregard, and she sucked in her pain and went with him.

"How you doing, baby?"

Beefy looked up at the helicopter pilot. A jigg ... They was everywhere ... buncha assholes.

"Hey, man," the black man said, "you know that is one fine car you got there ... I'll give you all my old back copies of *Ebony* magazine for that."

Beefy picked her up and helped her on board. He looked back at his car and felt his face redden. Shit, if he had had a Pontiac, everything would have been all right.

29

Cross moved down the halls, his OR greens on, his surgical mask pulled up over his face. In front of him he pushed the stretcher, with the white blanket over Sarah's drugged body. He stared at the cops who walked by him in the hall, at the nurses . . . and he thought as he went around the corner that if he took a left instead of a right, he would be able to walk right by Beauregard's station. They would all be in there, torturing themselves—wondering about him. But there would be no catching him now. He had them. He turned, opened the door to the Litt Building, and wheeled her in.

He turned and pulled out his keys. The room in front of him was dark, but he saw what he wanted inside. An operating table surrounded by tanks of cyclopropane, the most explosive gas in existence. OR Room 18 . . . seldom used anymore, due to a crack in the ceiling. They were going to fix it someday . . . but now it was fine for his purposes. Just fine. He wondered if they had found his car. He took her inside and cleared away some of the debris— an old anesthesia machine and a couple of tanks of oxygen. Then he locked the door behind him and pulled the shade down on the glass. Quickly he scooped her off the stretcher and placed her on the operating table. He smiled and prepared himself.

Operating Room 18 flashed into Beau's mind—of course—it was the only place possible.

"Shit—I know where he is," Beauregard said, as he and Lombardi began to trot down the corridor. Jimmy, Yvonne, and ten patrolmen hurried along behind them.

"It's been out of use for a while . . . the oldest one in the whole damned building."

"I think you're right, Doc," Lombardi said. "I'm beginning to think I know this guy. He wants an audience. This place . . . it's got an amphitheater?"

"Yes, it does . . . old-fashioned style. The place is like . . ."

"A theater," Lombardi said. "Do you see it? Everybody who kills nowadays thinks he is on a stage. Television, Doc. It's television. And worse, the newsboys will probably be here soon. Playing right up to him."

Beauregard looked over at Lombardi and shook his head.

"We've got to hurry," he said. "Come on . . . step it up."

They began to run, down the halls past open-mouthed patients, interrupted in the midst of dinner. Beauregard could feel his heart pounding inside him, and something else, which sounded very much like a child's scream.

He hooked up the cyclopropane tank, leaving the pop-off valve open. Then he looked at the spare tank and smiled. The gas was his ally. The gas and the Space, and it suddenly occurred to him that they were the same thing. They always had been . . . exactly the same. He picked up the other tank and placed it on the floor next to the operating table. Yes, the perfect place for it . . . Now if they tried any of that sharpshooter SWAT team bullshit, he would simply take her with him. One hit on that tank and it would crash to the floor, causing such an explosion that the entire room would be engulfed. And she would be a charred princess. He made ready with his potassium syringe, checked his paper slippers, the ones used to ground the static electricity . . . all set . . . yes, he was ready. Ready. Above him, the light went on.

Outside in the dawn, over a hundred New York City policemen surrounded Eastern Medical. In their hands were rifles, tear gas guns, and billy clubs. On their faces was a look of studied indifference. Enrico Estrada, a star newsman from "Hello America," ran from his mobile TV truck. On his way up the steps, he combed his hair and admired himself in a pocket mirror. Inside the lobby he ran into Jack Jacobs, of "NewsTeam Five."

"Enrico," Jack said. "You're looking good. Late, but good. I already got an exclusive interview with Beauregard, and the kid. If she makes it."

Enrico didn't even dignify the slob with a response. He had a lot more to offer. He was thinking pilots, mini-series, and spin-offs to prime-time TV. Residuals floated through his brain like aspirin through cartoon intestines.

"What floor?" he said to Jacobs.

"Four," he said. "It's a zoo up there, baby. Over fifty cops in the hallway. They aren't letting anybody through."

"What's the deal?"

"I don't know. He's holding her hostage."

"The kid?"

"Yeah . . . but it's strange. He hasn't asked for TV or anything."

"What's he, nuts?" Enrico laughed.

But he wasn't listening to Jacobs any longer. Behind him he heard sirens, and a minute later the police were rushing through the newspaper reporters who swarmed around them, and around a woman, a very battered, shell-shocked-looking blond with eyes as hard as marbles.

"See you later," Enrico said. He tagged along behind the cops, moving quickly and signaling to his TV crew to come up with him. The cameraman stayed on his tail, and the cops were too busy trying to push their way through the flashbulbs to notice him. Enrico smiled. Nothing had stopped him from getting a story. He was going to be out of the newsbeat soon—be a producer of a medical series, and this could be a big, big break. He had seen this guy Beauregard on Broadway. Maybe if the kid got killed, he could help the bereaved by asking the good doctor to host the show. That was a smart ploy. Yeah, "East Side Medical" . . . hosted by a head administrator of a "famous New York hospital." God, it was great. Probably get a fifty share in the ratings. He hugged tight to the backs of the police and kept moving. Soon they were in the elevators, on their way up.

Beauregard switched on the lights of the gallery and stared down on Peter Cross, and his daughter, strapped on the table beneath him. In a glance he saw the cyclopropane tanks, and turned to Lombardi and Heather, who stood by him.

"He's got cyclo," he said. "Tell your boys not to make any sudden moves . . . If anybody goes in there at all, and anything happens, it goes and Sarah goes with it."

He picked up the microphone, sitting on the blond wooden desk.

"All right, Cross, I'm here," he said. "This is the way you wanted it, isn't it."

He saw the man who held his daughter captive beneath him, and watched as that man smiled up at him, a terrifying smile, for Cross was in a position of absolute strength now. He had relinquished the burden of his humanity, and for the brief time that remained he was like a god. Beauregard looked and felt a terrible awe, a

204

chill in his gut. He thought of things that he had long forgotten . . . early classes in ethics taken as "guts" way back in the beginning of his university days. The urge to play God . . . the urge to destroy, as well as create. Classes that he had long forgotten . . . Christ, that was it . . . There could be no doubt . . . Only it was his child being used down there to act out the proposition. His only daughter. He heard Heather cry, and he turned and put his arm around her.

The he heard Cross's voice.

"What a touching scene," Cross said. "You and the Missus . . . together again . . . brought together by the threat of a lunatic. That's what you're thinking, hey, Beauregard? . . . A lunatic? . . . I'll bet in the future you and Mrs. Beauregard there—excuse me—Heather, will be able to sit down over some sole and have a serious talk about this. A little polite cocktail chatter, hey? Over some carrots and dip . . . a few drinks with a twist, hey? Only it's going to be a little tougher keeping the old good humor this time, isn't it . . . a little tougher because this time it's going to involve you, do you understand that? This time when you talk about the looney who is killing the patients at Eastern, the patient's going to be Sarah . . . You think you'll be able to keep a nice detached professional view of that?"

Cross stopped and heard his voice echoing through the room. A rather good speech, he thought . . . rather good . . . How he hated them all . . . hated them . . . But don't talk too long . . . for they were already massing at the door. They were talking to one another, signaling for men to lie down, to keep cool . . . He held the needle up for Beauregard to see.

"Potassium, Beauregard," he said. "And along the floor . . . cyclopropane. And little Sarah has no cyclo slippers. You know what will happen if I fall. Everything goes up.

You hear me, Doctor?"

"I hear you, Cross," Beauregard said. He wanted to leap through the window and land on the bastard, grab the needle from him, and plunge it into his face. "I hear you . . . You sound very angry, Peter . . . very angry . . . but I don't understand why. I thought you and I were friends."

Cross laughed loudly, flashing his needle like a sword.

Beauregard gripped the chair back in front of him.

"That's it, Doc," Lombardi said. "Keep talking to him."

"Where are you going?" Beauregard said.

"I'm going in there," Lombardi said. "It's time, Doc. We can't wait any longer."

"No," Heather said suddenly.

"No," Beauregard said, calm now. "No, you aren't going in . . . I am."

"Sorry, Doc."

"Sorry?" Beauregard said. "That's my daughter in there. This is . . . in some ways my fault . . . but there's only one of us he wants to see. If you make a move, he'll kill my daughter."

"And if you make a move, he'll kill you and your daughter," Lombardi said.

"Maybe," Beauregard said. "Just maybe . . . But maybe not, too."

"All right, Doc," Lombardi said. "We'll risk it . . . but I'll be right behind you."

Beauregard nodded and pressed Heather's hand. He picked up the hand mike.

"I'll be coming down now, Peter," he said, trying to sound as casual as possible.

Cross looked up and smiled at him.

"Come on, Doc," he said, "I've been waiting for this."

Beauregard turned, opened the door to the gallery, and walked out into the hall. Lombardi motioned to Heather.

206

"Listen," he said. "Stand there. Talk to him . . . slowly
. . . Don't say anything disturbing . . ."

She nodded and began.

"Peter," she said, "please don't hurt Sarah."

Beauregard worked his way down through the crowd.
The police had cordoned off the entire fourth floor, and
behind the wall of blue, he could see Yvonne, and then
June . . . and when he looked at them, their faces seemed
to melt . . . Then he was being grabbed at, handled.

"Hey, Dr. Beauregard, you going in there? I'm Enrico
Estrada, from 'Hello America'."

"Not now," Beauregard said.

"Hey, wait a minute, pal," Estrada said, sticking a mike
in Beauregard's face.

Beau pushed Estrada back, and the jaunty little re-
porter tripped over his own heels and fell against a cop,
who helped him by moving aside, leaving the little Latino
to crash to the floor.

This is it, Beauregard thought, slipping on the paper
slippers which would at least protect him from the deadly
gas.

"How lethal is that stuff, Doc?" Lombardi asked.

"Like this," Beauregard said.

He scratched his nail on the green tile wall.

"One good scrape and it's all she wrote."

"Take it slow, Doc."

Lombardi reached up and patted him on the shoulder.
Then they moved aside, and he started for the door.

Cross unlocked the door, stepped back into the room,
then he saw him coming toward him now . . . shuffling his
feet like a little old man. It was amusing . . . infinitely
amusing how weak they were. There was nothing to their
might. He recalled how, in the old days, a stern look from

Beauregard at an M and M meeting would depress him for days, and he couldn't resist laughing out loud.

"How you doing, Doc?" he said.

Beauregard sized him up, then stopped.

"I'm fine, Peter," he said, "I'm just fine... How are you doing?"

"Terrific," Cross said. "I've never felt better."

"You feel good, Peter?"

"Except about Debby," Peter said, suddenly sober. "I feel bad about Debby... that was your fault, Dr. Beauregard... It really was... I didn't want to hurt her, but I had to protect myself—protect my patients."

Beauregard took another step forward. He could smell the gas all around him, and he watched as Cross stood over his daughter, holding the syringe over her, her arm in his hand.

"I can understand that, Peter," he said.

"Can you?" Cross said. "How could you understand how I felt?"

Beau made a quick decision—he had an audience— an audience that would hear what he'd been keeping in his gut for years.

"I understand you, Peter, because we're a lot alike."

"That's what I always liked about you, Dr. Beauregard ... you're straight... dull but straight. Your options are so black and white."

"Not *that* dull, Peter. You think you're the only one who's killed a patient?"

Cross stopped.

"You?"

Beauregard nodded again, slowly, three times.

"Twice," Beauregard said. "Twice..."

Cross let the needle up a bit. He was slack-jawed.

"Twice," Beauregard said. "One was an old man...

208

he had so little time left anyway, it was easy to let him go."

Cross had begun to sweat a little.

"You're lying."

Beauregard advanced a step, shook his head.

"No," he said. "The second was a young girl . . . not much older than Sarah. She was thirteen and she had leukemia. So many tests, so many pints of blood, so many treatments . . . She had days—maybe a week. She didn't want to go on . . . so I let her out . . . Isn't that it, Peter . . . You want to let them out . . . Let them run free of their bodies . . . Isn't that it?"

Cross was nodding, slowly. He was shaking badly.

"You see," Beauregard said, moving forward, only two feet away from him, "I'm not that dull . . . nor do I hate you . . . I'm still your friend, Peter . . . You need friends."

Cross nodded, and Beauregard started to move forward again. But now Cross's eyes lit up, and he grabbed Sarah again.

"You are lying," he said. "You have to be."

"I don't lie," Beauregard said.

Cross blinked, ran his tongue around his dry lips.

"But if what you say is true," Cross said, "then we're the same . . . you and I, exactly the same."

Beauregard shook his head again.

"No," he said, "we're not the same. Because when I killed, I didn't celebrate. I forgot. You see?"

Cross's eyes opened wide, and he gave out a startled cry. Then Beauregard was on him.

Cross screamed and hit Beauregard on the left temple, knocking him back. He moved toward Sarah, grabbing her arm, nearly getting the needle in, but Beauregard grabbed him and flung him across the room. Cross fell in the corner next to some old oxygen tanks. Beauregard grabbed Sarah in his arms and started for the door. Then he looked at his feet. The electrical grounding slipper had fallen off in the fight. He proceeded slowly . . . the door looked as though it were receding. He made it halfway across the room before Cross was on him, seizing him by the neck and pulling him back. Sarah fell to the floor, smashing her head, and Beauregard pushed hard, back into Peter, driving both of them down. He shot an elbow into Cross's ribs, then he turned and smashed Cross in the face. But still Cross wouldn't go down. He grabbed Beauregard's lapel and tried to jam the needle into his cheek. Beauregard grasped his wrist and pulled it back, and Cross pressed forward.

"The eyes," he said. "In the eyes . . ."

Beauregard caught his leg behind him and pushed him down on the floor. Cross fell backward and reached for the empty tank of cyclopropane. He grabbed it and started to grasp it again.

Beauregard watched it happen. He saw Lombardi's hands reach out for Sarah. Heard the deafening blast, saw the red and blue flames. Then he turned and tried to cover his daughter who had been knocked to the floor. But he himself was thrown backward, blasted up against the wall . . . and he heard her scream out . . . and saw the flames again. Then he was gone, porous as gas.

Epílogue

"You don't have to do this," Debby said, as they sped along the Interborough Expressway.

Beauregard and Heather both turned around in the front seat, and Debby couldn't help but stare at Beau's bandaged right hand.

"No," Beauregard said, "I want to."

Heather smiled, and turned her attention back to the driving.

"Me too," Sarah said, stretching out her left leg. The right one was still tightly bandaged. The doctors had done good work on her, and she was going to be all right … but the pain was still there. Both she and Beau had been lucky. Neither had been too seriously burned.

"Well, it's just that I guess it seems crazy," Debby said. "It isn't often anyone goes to visit the grave of the person that tried to kill them."

"That's true," Heather said. "If the papers got hold of this story, it would be on page one."

"I know," Debby said. "I know it …"

She looked out the window at the sparse trees on the side of the road. Some of them were actually beginning to bud, and on the ground beneath them she saw a patch of daisys. Up above them the sky was blue, and she let out a long sigh.

"It's just that there were very few people like Peter

Cross . . . I mean . . . in spite of what he did . . . to me and the others. I feel sorry about it. No, that wasn't it. Not sorry. I feel as though his death was really tragic."

"I understand, Debby," Sarah said. "He was a real brain."

The car turned off the little dirt road, and they went under the big sign which said Cypress Hills in black iron scrollwork.

When they passed through the wrought iron gate, Debby felt cold and foolish. She wondered what she herself would say if someone had told her they were going to visit the grave of the man who had tried to kill them. It was ghoulish, definitely very unliberated. She stared out the window at the hundreds of tombstones, the crypts, the vaults . . . and she thought that if you dwelt on it, if you picked out that one fact from all the others, that this was where it all ended up, then really what difference did anything make? She looked again and saw it the way Peter had . . . peaceful, beyond struggle, perfect. She had finally started to understand his view of it. After four months of thinking about it, after waking up with the cold sweats in the middle of the night, waiting for the hands to come down on her again, thinking of his leering face, something had happened . . . a breakthrough of a kind (although some people would probably call it a breakdown) . . . she had finally understood—at least as much as possible—Peter Cross's motivations. And understanding them, while not reducing the horror of what he did, made it real for her. Humanly real. And being human, not merely a gothic fantasy, made it bearable. For he had acted perversely out of love. She saw that now, everything he had done had been out of love. Of course that was too simple . . . a blanket which covered an endless tapestry of subtle, but massive lies . . .

The car stopped, and Beauregard pointed to a lonely-

212

looking hill, where amidst a few patches of green grass and a couple of blue flowers, a single stone stood.

"I'm staying in the car," Sarah said. "I was wrong to come out here. It's still too scary for me."

"Okay," Heather said, "you need to rest that leg anyway, "but you do see that Peter Cross is buried there. Those nightmares you've been having are just that . . . dreams. He's not coming to get you."

"I see," Sarah said.

"Good," Heather said, patting her arm. "Will you be all right here while we go up there?"

"Sure," Sarah said.

They got out of the car and walked up the hill. Beauregard took both of their arms. When they stopped, he read the headstone.

Peter Cross   1943–1979   Physician

"That's nice," Debby said, trying not to cry. "There's a part of him, you know, that would have liked that."

"I know," Beauregard said. "I guess I came here today for a reason too. It's not that I blame myself, because the damage to Peter had been done a long, long time ago. But still, I feel in some way responsible."

"He wanted perfection," Debby said.

Beauregard nodded.

"Yes, and innocence. He was able to kill because he was in love with the idea of innocence, of purity . . . perhaps more than anything else. Maybe it was ideas that did him in. The idea of a lost perfect love, twisted and turned black by his own self-hatred—the terrible loathing of his own mortal body."

"Perhaps now he has found peace," Heather said.

"Maybe," Beauregard said. "Whatever it is, it's what he really wanted."

Debby took a deep breath and placed the lilies across his grave.

"Good-bye, Peter," she said.

Then the three of them turned and went down the hill toward the car.

Beauregard and Heather climbed in the front, Debby in the back. She looked down at Sarah, curled up on the seat.

"She looks just like an angel," Debby said.

Heather and Beauregard turned and smiled down at their child.

"They always do," Beauregard said, "when they're asleep."

9 781440 555053